"I'd like you to leave now."

"Yeah, I know, I can see that in your eyes." His smile was quick and dangerous. "How about what I'd like?"

"I don't care what you'd…"

The words died in her throat when he dipped his head and brushed her lips with his.

Her eyes went wide and stayed that way, fixed on his. She didn't blink, didn't move.

Against her lips he murmured, "You're supposed to breathe."

She couldn't. Nor could she think. Instead, she stood, frozen in place, as the most amazing splinters of fire and ice danced through her veins.

He nuzzled her lips. She tasted like summer rain. All cool and clean and fresh. The effect was startling.

Though ⬛⬛⬛⬛⬛⬛⬛⬛ pounds, he coul⬛ ⬛⬛⬛⬛⬛⬛⬛mbination of shoc⬛ ⬛⬛⬛⬛⬛⬛⬛ence unbeli⬛⬛ ⬛⬛⬛⬛⬛facade he could tas⬛⬛ ⬛⬛⬛⬛⬛t and sweet.

For the first time in ages he found himself wanting to forget all the rules and simply take and take until he was filled with this woman.

Dear Reader,

Once again we invite you to enjoy six of the most
exciting romances around, starting with Ruth Langan's
His Father's Son. This is the last of THE LASSITER LAW,
her miniseries about a family with a tradition of law
enforcement, and it's a finale that will leave you looking
forward to this bestselling author's next novel. Meanwhile,
enjoy Cameron Lassiter's headlong tumble into love.

ROMANCING THE CROWN continues with
Virgin Seduction, by award winner Kathleen Creighton.
The missing prince is home at last—and just in time
for the shotgun wedding between Cade Gallagher and
Tamiri princess Leila Kamal. Carla Cassidy continues
THE DELANEY HEIRS with Matthew's story, in
Out of Exile, while Pamela Dalton spins a tale of a couple
who are *Strategically Wed*. Sharon Mignerey returns with
an emotional tale of a hero who is *Friend, Lover, Protector*,
and Leann Harris wraps up the month with a match between
The Detective and the D.A.

You won't want to miss a single one. And, of course, be
sure to come back next month for more of the most exciting
romances around—right here in Silhouette Intimate Moments.

Enjoy!

Leslie J. Wainger
Executive Senior Editor

Please address questions and book requests to:
Silhouette Reader Service
U.S.: 3010 Walden Ave., P.O. Box 1325, Buffalo, NY 14269
Canadian: P.O. Box 609, Fort Erie, Ont. L2A 5X3

His Father's
Son
RUTH LANGAN

INTIMATE MOMENTS™

Published by Silhouette Books

America's Publisher of Contemporary Romance

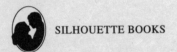

SILHOUETTE BOOKS

ISBN 0-373-27217-0

HIS FATHER'S SON

Copyright © 2002 by Ruth Ryan Langan

This edition published by arrangement with Harlequin Books S.A.

® and TM are trademarks of Harlequin Books S.A., used under license.
Trademarks indicated with ® are registered in the United States Patent
and Trademark Office, the Canadian Trade Marks Office and in other
countries.

Visit Silhouette at www.eHarlequin.com

Printed in U.S.A.

Books by Ruth Langan

RUTH LANGAN

is an award-winning and bestselling author. Her books have been finalists for the Romance Writers of America's RITA® Award. Over the years, she has given dozens of print, radio and TV interviews, including *Good Morning America* and *CNN News,* and has been quoted in such diverse publications as *The Wall Street Journal, Cosmopolitan* and *The Detroit Free Press.* Married to her childhood sweetheart, she has raised five children and lives in Michigan, the state where she was born and raised.

Here's to families everywhere
who laugh and tease and offer love and support
and a place to celebrate this wonderful life.

Here's to my own large and loving family,
quick with a joke or a hug,
who make me laugh and keep me grounded.

And especially to Tom,
who started it all in first grade.

Prologue

Chevy Chase, Maryland, 1986

Kieran Lassiter's footsteps echoed in the empty hallway of the Brighton Military Academy. When he stepped into the school office a dark-haired woman looked up, then gave him a welcoming smile.

"Mr. Lassiter. Commander Trilby is expecting you."

Kieran was a master at exuding Irish charm when it was needed. This was definitely a day that required all the charm he could muster.

He winked. "Miss Lacey, you wouldn't happen to know what this meeting is about now, would you?"

"I'm afraid it wouldn't be proper for me to comment."

He leaned close, wearing his best conspiratorial smile. The hair may have been silver, but there was a young rogue in those midnight-blue eyes. "Then you don't have to say a thing. Just answer yes or no. Has my grandson Cameron been fighting again?"

She blushed and nodded.

Kieran winced. It was the lad's third offense, which could mean he was being expelled. Again. The boy had gone from public school to private school to military school, and none had been able to reach that angry place inside him since the day his father had been ripped from his young life.

After Kieran's son Riordan had been killed in the line of duty, the Lassiter family had struggled to find their way. Kate, a young widow with four children, had led them all with such strength, the others had naturally followed along. But not without pitfalls. Kieran, himself a retired police officer, had moved in to take over the cooking and cleaning chores, in order to free Kate to return to college, and now, to law school. Each of the four children had presented the old man with their share of challenges. But Cameron, the youngest, seemed determined to wear him down. He was a lost boy. Angry. Confused. With such a fire inside him the slightest spark could set him off.

"Will the commander give him another chance?"

The school secretary looked truly apologetic. "I know Commander Trilby has great regard for the Lassiter name and reputation. But as you know, he's a stickler for the rules of the academy."

Kieran nodded. "I was afraid of that. My thanks, Miss Lacey."

She pressed the intercom on her desk. "Commander, Mr. Kieran Lassiter is here to see you."

Kieran straightened his tie before opening the door and stepping into the commander's office.

"Mr. Lassiter." The man behind the desk stood military straight, his uniform as crisp as when he'd put it on ten hours earlier. "Have a seat."

"Thank you." Kieran sat down in one of the two straight-backed chairs facing the desk.

Without preamble the commander said, "I knew about Cameron's temper when I accepted his application to Brighton. And I suppose I was vain enough to believe that we could make a difference. Today, after three detentions, the dean of discipline was forced to give Cameron another one when he engaged two upperclassmen in a fistfight."

Kieran waited for the shoe to drop.

"I think you should see this." The commander opened a drawer and removed a sheaf of papers, which he passed across his desk.

Kieran glanced at them, then looked over. "I thought this was about fighting."

"It is. In a manner of speaking." The commander pointed. "This test measures not only intelligence, but potential, as well. On the last page of that report, you'll see your grandson's rating, compared with that of other students his age."

Kieran flipped to the last page and stared in disbelief at the figures. He glanced at the commander, as if for confirmation of what he'd read.

Commander Trilby folded his hands, steepling

his fingers. "Cameron has one of the highest scores of any student who has ever taken these tests. He has unlimited potential. But until we can get him to play by the rules, to move beyond his anger, or at least to find a more appropriate outlet for that anger, all his talents are being wasted."

Kieran sighed. "I take it you're saying that my grandson has no place in the Brighton Military Academy?"

The commander shook his head. "What I'm saying is that I'd be willing to make an exception in Cameron's case. I will give him another chance, providing he can be persuaded to follow the rules to the letter."

Kieran felt a flicker of hope. He'd been dreading the thought of having to give Kate the news that her youngest son had gone down for the count a third time.

He got to his feet and reached a hand across the desk. "Thank you, Commander. Where is my grandson?"

"In the gym. I asked him how he worked off his aggression at home, and he said you made him shoot hoops."

Kieran nodded. "It's been my rule for as long as I've been with him and his family."

"I told him he would have to remain there, working off his anger, until you came to claim him." As Kieran reached for the door the commander added, "It is imperative that you find a way to reach your grandson, Mr. Lassiter. It would be a crime to see such potential go to waste. But I cannot and will not allow him to continue on here at Brighton unless he agrees to my terms."

Kieran strode down the hall. When he stepped inside the gym he saw Cameron on the far side. The boy dribbled, made the layup, then watched as the ball dropped neatly through the hoop. He caught the ball, drove hard and took it up again. The minute it dropped, he went through the same punishing ritual again and again.

Just watching him made the old man tired. There was such restlessness in the boy. Such passion and fury.

When he turned and caught sight of his grandfather, he tossed the ball aside and picked up a towel, drying himself as he crossed the court. His face was flushed, his chest heaving from the workout. The anger was still there, simmering in those stormy blue eyes.

Kieran was silent as he studied the bruise on his grandson's cheek.

Seeing the way his grandfather was taking his measure, Cameron frowned. "I can have my locker cleaned out in a couple of minutes."

Kieran shook his head. "Not so fast, boyo."

He paused, the towel halfway to his face. "I know the rules. I'm out of here."

"Is that why you picked a fight? To get yourself tossed from another school?"

When the boy lifted his chin like a boxer and clenched his jaw, Kieran felt a sudden jolt of pain at the memory of another. His voice lowered. "You're like him, you know."

Cam's eyes blazed. "Are you talking about my father?"

Kieran nodded. "You look like him. Fight like him. You even sound like him."

The boy turned away. "How would I know? I can't even remember him. When you and Mom and the others talk about him, I feel like you're talking about a stranger."

"That stranger loved you."

"Yeah. He loved me so much he got himself killed."

"You think your father wanted to die, boyo?" Kieran closed a hand around Cameron's arm, spinning him around to face him. The old man struggled to bank the pain that crept into his tone. "Is that what all this fighting is about? Are you mad at your own father all these years because he dared to die and leave you?"

Cam looked away and held his silence. It spoke more than words.

Kieran's voice was a low hiss of controlled passion. "Now let me tell you something, boyo. Your father was so damned proud of you. I thought the day you were born, he'd bust all the buttons off his uniform. He was passing around your picture at the police station and handing out the finest cigars. And do you know what he told me?"

Cameron lowered his head, but not before Kieran saw the flicker of interest in his eyes.

"He said, Pop, this one's going to be the strongest, smartest, toughest Lassiter of all." Kieran's voice lowered. "And you are, Cameron. You're all your father hoped you'd be. You're stronger than your brother Micah.

Tougher than your brother Donovan. And smarter than your sister, Mary Brendan. You're strong and smart and tough. Maybe too tough for your own good. You see, none of those things by themselves are enough.'' He cleared his throat. ''Commander Trilby is willing to give you another chance.''

Cam's head came up, doubt, suspicion and anger all warring in his eyes. ''Why?''

''Because he sees something in you. Something special. And so do I, boyo. But if you get into another fight, it'll be your last.''

Cam was already shaking his head. ''I can't promise…''

''Yes, you can.'' Kieran's tone sharpened. ''If you're as smart as I think you are, you'll figure out that there's a better way to beat your opponent than by using your fists.''

''What's that supposed to mean? How can I fight without my fists?''

Kieran held up a hand to silence him. ''Think about this, boyo. The best way of all to beat your opponent is by using your brain.''

He could see his grandson digesting this.

Cam lifted his head. ''I don't know. I suppose I could try.''

Kieran clapped a hand on his grandson's shoulder. "That's my boy. You think you can keep your fists out of other people's faces, at least while you're here in school?"

Cam shrugged. "I suppose. As long as I can use them once in a while on Micah and Donovan at home."

Kieran threw back his head and roared. "I don't think you'd better try it for a few years yet, boyo. They've got fifty or sixty pounds over you."

"But not for long, Pop. When I'm all grown up, I'll take them both on."

"I've no doubt of that." The old man put an arm around his grandson's shoulders, feeling as though the weight of the world had just been lifted from his own. "Come on. Let's go home. I've a dinner to make."

As they settled themselves in the car Kieran said, "By the way, boyo. Commander Trilby said you fought with upperclassmen. What was this fight about?"

Cam turned to look out the window. "They said the only good cop was a dead one. I told them my dad was a cop who took a bullet meant for his partner and I wanted them to take back their words. When they wouldn't, I laid into them.''

''Who won?''

Cam's smile was pure Lassiter. ''You don't even need to ask, Pop. You ought to see their shiners.''

The man and boy rode the rest of the way home in silence. But Kieran made a promise to himself. The biggest slice of devil's food cake would go to this lad tonight. It was another thing Cameron shared with his dead father. Riordan Lassiter had been known for having the quickest fists in town. As well as a fondness for anything sweet.

Sometimes when the old man looked at this lad, he saw Riordan, back from the grave. The same handsome Irish face. The same quick grin. And a zeal to make things right, no matter what the cost.

But Cameron had something more. If the test results were to be believed, he'd been blessed with an amazing mind, as well.

Kieran decided that his one mission in life was to see that Cameron, the youngest of the Lassiter clan, reached his full potential. If he had anything to say about it, it would be the lad's brain that ruled his life, not his fists.

Chapter 1

"Sure, Martin. I can meet you at your club. Two o'clock tomorrow?" Cameron Lassiter made a notation on his desk calendar. "See you there."

He disconnected and buzzed his assistant. "Kathy, I'm meeting Martin O'Hara at Burning Tree tomorrow at two. Any conflict?"

The voice came over the intercom. "Three would have been better. You're meeting Mr. VanDorn for lunch. You know how he loves to drag out those luncheon meetings."

Cam sighed. "Yeah. I'll just have to get him to talk faster. Any messages?"

"Just one. Your mother asked that you phone her at her office."

"Thanks." Cam picked up the phone and punched in the familiar number. As the phone at the other end rang, he glanced around, thinking of the contrast between his office and that of his mother. Though they were both lawyers, their practices were at opposite ends of the spectrum. His firm, Stern Hayes Wheatley, handled the most prestigious clients in the country. A president, a former king and dozens of political figures had been served by the firm. As one of their top lawyers, Cameron Lassiter routinely won multimillion-dollar settlements, not to mention accolades for his brilliant courtroom technique, which was a cross between mortal combat and gentle persuasion.

He'd never outgrown his love of a good, satisfying fight.

His office, a stone's throw from the seat of power, reflected old money. Plush carpeting. Walls paneled in imported teak. On a sideboard, a Waterford pitcher and tumblers. The conference rooms boasted the latest in technology, offering an opportunity to see and speak with anyone in the world.

After graduating law school, Cam's mother had become a family advocate, opening an office in the poorest section of the district. Kate Lassiter's days were spent helping clients, many of whom were illiterate, to find their way through a maze of paperwork in order to secure basic necessities such as rent payments, medical help, food stamps.

Anyone who saw Cameron Lassiter, in his custom-tailored suits and flashy car, would be astounded to learn that he routinely did pro bono work for his mother. To date, he'd taken over a dozen cases, once considered beyond hope, and had their convictions overturned.

"Kate Lassiter."

"Hi, Mom." At the sound of her voice Cam leaned back in his chair. "How's your day going?"

She sighed. "Don't ask."

"That good, huh?" He fiddled with the gold pen on his desk. "How can I help?"

He heard the smile come into her voice. "You know me so well, Cam. I have this family. Actually, it's a grandmother and her grandson. The boy's mother hasn't been around in years. Apparently she left the boy with his grandmother and took off for parts unknown.''

''You want me to find her?''

''No. There's another family member. The boy has a father in prison. I wonder if you'd mind looking at his file.''

''What's his crime?''

Kate paused just a beat before saying, ''He was convicted of killing a police officer.''

Cam's voice hardened. ''I can't believe you'd even consider this, Mom.''

The silence stretched out between them before Kate sighed. ''Will you be coming by tonight for dinner?''

Cam glanced at his calendar and noted a meeting with the decorator at his new house in Virginia. ''I think so.''

''Would you mind if I brought the case file?''

It was Cam's turn to sigh. ''You can bring it, but I won't promise to read it.''

''I understand.'' Over a commotion in the background Kate could be heard saying, ''I have to go. I'll see you at home.''

Cam hung up the phone and sat a moment, eyes narrowed in thought. The sudden, wrenching pain caught him by surprise. It had been nearly twenty-five years since his father's life had been snuffed out by a thug's bullet. Yet he could remember the days that followed as vividly as though they'd happened yesterday. The funeral, with its honor guard and twenty-one-gun salute that left his heart pounding. The tears in his grandfather's eyes. The stoic way his mother had herded her family through the crowds of celebrities who had come to pay their respects. And later, the way the family stopped talking whenever he came into the room. He now understood that they'd only been trying to shield a five-year-old from the realities of life. What they'd failed to understand was that even at that tender age, he was grieving as deeply as they were, but was unable to express that grief.

His hands fisted at his sides as he stood and shoved back his chair. There was almost nothing he wouldn't do for his mother. But this time she was asking too much.

He'd be damned if he'd defend a cop killer.

"About time you got here, bro." Micah Lassiter clapped a hand on Cam's shoulder the minute he stepped into the kitchen.

Across the room Micah's wife, Pru, was stirring something on the stove.

Cam glanced around at the familiar chaos.

Meals at the Lassiter home were never quiet or simple. His brother Donovan was showing his son, Cory, how to grate cheese over steaming asparagus. Donovan's wife, Andi, was coaching their daughter, Taylor, in the proper way to skim gravy. Mary Brendan, now a member of the U.S. Congress, was mashing potatoes. Her husband, Chris, who had just been promoted to assistant police chief in D.C., was slicing a loaf of freshly baked bread. In the midst of it all was Kieran Lassiter, like a proud old lion, with that mane of white hair and those laughing blue eyes, carving a roast of beef.

"Stash that briefcase and fancy jacket, boyo." He waved his carving knife like a sword. "We need someone with your fine legal expertise to toss the salad."

Donovan burst into laughter. "I always knew that brain would be good for something."

Cam grinned as he walked into the great room and disposed of his attaché case and suit jacket. Rolling his sleeves, he returned to the noise of the kitchen and plunged into his chore. This was just what he needed to forget the cares of the day. His client, Lou Carlson, had been a tedious windbag. And the long-legged, gorgeous paralegal in the D.A.'s office, who was supposed to meet him later for drinks, had begged off because an old classmate had just arrived in D.C. Cam was willing to bet the old classmate was also an old boyfriend. Not that it mattered. There had been no sparks between them. Still, she was easy on the eye and made for a pleasant diversion.

Sometimes when he looked at his siblings, he couldn't help envying them the partners they'd found. Each of them seemed to bring something unique and special to the family. He doubted he'd ever meet someone who could fit in with the very loud and very opinionated Lassiters.

By the time Kate walked in, the laughter and easy banter had escalated to a roar.

"I saw you on TV this afternoon, Bren." Micah winked at Donovan, prepared to tease his sister about her newly acquired fame. "Now about this bill you're proposing. Do I understand that our esteemed members of Congress now hope to control even our garbage?"

That had everyone howling with laughter.

Bren's answering smile was forced. "Maybe you don't care that this country is drowning in garbage, but I do. And I intend to do something about it."

"You realize the media has already dubbed it

the Lassiter Garbage Bill.'' Donovan kept a straight face. ''Now there's something to wear with pride.''

''I'll have you know...'' Bren's words faded when her husband drew an arm around her shoulders and whispered in her ear.

She pushed away. ''Of course I know they're having fun at my expense. It's the Lassiter way. But I have a right to defend my position.''

''And your garbage,'' Cam muttered as he mixed precise amounts of vinegar and oil like a chemist.

Bren was about to argue the point when Chris whispered something more that had her blushing.

''You care to share, little sis?'' Micah was grinning like a fool. ''Or have you two suddenly decided that you have to leave right after dinner?''

''Leave your sister alone, Micah.'' Pru stepped close and linked her arm with his.

''Yes, dear. Anything you say, dear.'' He grinned and brushed a kiss over her cheek.

''Which translates into, 'Let's follow Chris and Bren's lead and ditch the family as soon as possible.''' Donovan's words had the entire family laughing.

Kate kicked off her shoes and settled herself at the big trestle table, letting the sights and sounds of her family wash over her. This was what she needed at the end of a long, challenging day. Just the knowledge that she could return to this place, and this tightly knit clan, made all the work worthwhile.

Kieran placed a cup of tea in front of her. "You're quiet tonight, Katie girl."

"Just a bit tired. But this restores me."

He nodded. "I know what you mean."

It wasn't long before the meal had been carried into the dining room and the entire family was gathered around the table.

As they took their places, they linked hands while Kieran intoned the words they'd heard since childhood. "Bless this food and those gathered here to share it. And bless Riordan, who watches over us all."

Cameron glanced at his mother and saw her eyes close for just a moment at the mention of her dead husband. It had been her strength that had kept them all going after their terrible loss. Where had that great well of strength come from?

Bren turned to Cameron. "I heard your firm mentioned today in connection with the Mc-

Gonnagle-Carlson case. They're talking about millions of dollars. Have you heard who's going to be assigned to it?''

Cam nodded. "Yeah. Looks like I drew the short straw.''

"You?''

Everyone at the table was staring at him.

"When were you going to tell us, boyo?'' Kieran's smile spread across his face.

"I figured I'd get around to it sooner or later.'' Cam buttered a slice of bread before glancing at his sister. "And it isn't for millions. The winner will get more than a billion dollars in the final settlement.''

Even Donovan, who always managed to turn everything into a joke, looked impressed.

Micah lifted his cup of tea. "Here's to you, little brother.''

The others followed suit, lifting glasses of milk and cups of tea.

Cam winked at his nephew, Cory. "Don't let all this fool you. Did you hear what your uncle Micah called me? They still think of me as the baby of the family.''

"Not any more, bro.'' Micah glanced around at the others, who were smiling and nodding. "I'd say you've made it to the big time.''

Across the table Kate smiled at her son. "This is a grand honor, Cameron. I know you'll win this case for your firm."

He laughed. "If I don't, I may be looking for a job."

Pru spoke up. "If that happens, I know the perfect place."

When the others looked at her she added, "I happen to know a certain family advocate who is swamped with work. I've heard from our case-workers at Children's Village that Kate's office does more for the disadvantaged of the city than any government agency."

Kate blushed. "I think you're exaggerating, Pru."

"Not at all. Every day I come into contact with people singing your praises, Kate. They claim without the work you do, they would have no one to turn to for help in this big, impersonal city."

"I do my best." Kate ducked her head and finished her tea.

After thick slices of carrot cake and many cups of tea, the family began clearing the table. While the dining room grew quiet, the noise level in the kitchen grew to a roar.

Micah loaded plates in the dishwasher.

"How's that big, fancy house in Virginia coming, little brother?"

"I met with the decorator again. Everything's in place except for the king-size bed. It had to be custom-ordered."

"Judging by the time it's taken you, I thought everything in that mansion was being customized." Donovan grinned at his wife. "Seems to me you've been almost a year in getting it the way you want it. Are you sure this is a house? Or maybe you're designing yourself a monument."

"I like things neat."

"Is that so?" Micah tossed him a wet dishrag. "That makes you the perfect candidate for cleaning up the dining room table."

While the others laughed, Cam stepped into the dining room and wiped down the table. That finished, he looked toward a light in the great room. Kate sat at a desk, where a file folder lay open.

He walked up beside her. "Homework?"

"Yeah." She looked up smiling. "It never ends, does it?"

He shook his head and began to read over her shoulder.

"Who is Tio Johnson?"

"The boy I told you about. He lives with his grandmother. She's worried she's going to lose him. The authorities have threatened to take him away because he's missed so much school."

"Why is he missing school?"

Kate shrugged. "Instead of going to class, he hitches rides to McCutchin Prison to visit his father. Then he hitches rides back home, sometimes after dark."

Cam frowned. "Sounds like the grandmother needs to have a little better control of the kid."

Kate sat back and looked at her son. "You mean, the way your grandfather and I had control of you when you were constantly getting into fights."

Cam crossed his arms over his chest. "That was different."

"How?"

"I wasn't hitching rides to prison to visit a convicted killer."

"No. You were getting kicked out of one school after another. Picking fights with boys twice your size to prove how tough you were. And as I recall, doing it all because you were mad at the whole world."

Cam's eyes narrowed. "You think I'm going

to see some connection between this kid and me?''

Kate shook her head. ''Of course not. What possible similarity could there be between you, a privileged boy who'd lost his father to death, and a boy from the ghetto who's lost his father to prison?'' She turned away. ''Now I'd better get back to work.''

He reached over her shoulder and picked up the file folder. ''I want to read this.''

She looked up. ''Why?''

He shrugged. ''Maybe to prove to you and to myself that what happens to this kid and his family is no concern of mine.''

''Fine. Read it.'' She watched as he headed for the stairs. ''You aren't going home tonight?''

He shook his head. The house he'd bought, in the rolling Virginia countryside, was being completely refurbished by one of the area's top decorating firms. The minute he'd seen the spacious rooms, the big, open fireplace, the rolling acres of lawn, he'd vowed to make it his. And though it now boasted fresh paint and carpeting, and rooms filled with exquisite furniture, Cam didn't want to move in until everything was just right. At least that's what he told himself.

"The bed I ordered still hasn't been delivered. I'm going up to my old room."

Kate pointed with her pen. "See that I get Tio's file back before you leave in the morning."

Cameron was at the door of his old apartment above the garage before it hit him. His mother knew him so well. She'd known, of course, that he could never resist a challenge, whether it was with his fists or his mind. And so she'd set him up perfectly.

He sighed. As long as he had the file, he'd read it. But nothing would change his mind. He didn't care how sad this kid's story was, Cam had no intention of wasting his time and energy on a cop killer.

He turned on the bedside lamp and plumped up the pillow before settling down to read.

Chapter 2

Hearing no morning sounds in the kitchen, Cam picked up his attaché case from the hall table. The moment he stepped through the doorway, he realized his mistake. Kieran was at the stove, turning bacon. Kate was at the table, sipping coffee.

Both looked up as he entered.

"Sit down, boyo." Kieran started filling a plate with bacon and scrambled eggs.

"Sorry, Pop. I don't have time."

"You'll make time." It was an argument they'd waged since Cam was a boy. Kieran expected everyone to start the day with fuel. In this case, enough food to feed an army.

"Look, Pop…"

"Sit. Your breakfast is getting cold." Kieran set the plate on the table and returned to the stove for the coffee.

Across the table Kate merely rolled her eyes and bit into toast.

Defeated, as he knew he would be, Cam dropped his attaché case onto a chair and tucked into his meal. After several bites he cleared his throat. "I have Tio's file. Interesting bedtime reading." He unsnapped his case and handed his mother the manila folder. He waited a beat before asking, "What will you recommend to his caseworker?"

"That he be allowed to remain in the custody of his grandmother. But I fear I'll have little influence. She wants him taken from his grandmother's care and placed in a juvenile facility until they determine whether or not she's fit to care for the boy."

Cam's head came up. "Why a juvenile facility?"

"So he can't run away again and hitch a ride to prison."

"Oh, great. And in the meantime, the kid will be stuck in a place with delinquents, trouble-makers and juvenile criminals. I'll bet that'll teach him." His voice lowered. "Does this case-worker really believe a juvenile facility will hold that kid?"

"She considers it a better alternative than living with a grandmother who can't make him behave."

"Oh, he'll behave in juvie, all right. Until the first chance he gets to break free. Then he'll end up living on the street."

Kate sipped her coffee. "It sounds as though Tio Johnson is getting to you."

Cam shook his head. "He's just a name in a file. But the file makes him out to be a criminal, when all he really is a twelve-year-old kid who wants to see his father."

Kate shrugged. "My hands are tied, Cameron. I can recommend that he remain with his grand-mother, but the boy's caseworker will have the final say."

Cam shoved away from the table and tossed down his napkin. "Well, my hands aren't tied. I'm not going to stand by and watch some smug little social worker take this kid away from the only steadying influence in his life. I may not approve of his father, but that doesn't mean I won't fight for the kid.''

''You're taking up Tio's cause?''

He paused at the door. ''Just watch me.''

Cam parked his car outside the dingy offices his mother shared with an overworked, underpaid staff. He and his brothers had spent a weekend last summer painting the walls of the office in bright colors, while his sister had added pretty touches like plants and silk flowers. Now, though the plants thrived, the silk flowers were faded and the walls were chipped and peeling. He felt a measure of guilt for the plush office he enjoyed at Stern Hayes Wheatley.

His mother's smile, when she caught sight of him, more than made up for the drab surroundings.

''Cameron. What a surprise.'' Kate was on her feet and in the doorway as he threaded his way between the desks.

Most of the women in the office may have been past fifty, but they still cast admiring glances at the handsome man in the charcoal suit and dove-gray silk tie.

Kate gave a delighted laugh. "I thought you had a full calendar."

"I did." He pressed a kiss to her cheek and noticed the young woman seated across from his mother's desk. Drab suit, but great legs. He shot her a smile before turning to Kate. "Luckily my last client of the day canceled. So I thought I'd get started on Tio's case and see what ammunition to use against his idiot caseworker."

Kate felt the heat rise to her cheeks. "Cameron, I'd like you to meet Summer O'Connor."

"Summer. My friends call me Cam." He gave her one of his killer smiles, guaranteed to melt the heart of any female within range. "How nice to meet you."

"I doubt you'll think that in a moment." The young woman froze him with a glacial look. "I'm Tio Johnson's idiot caseworker."

Kate had the good sense to discreetly leave so Cam could dig himself deeper or find a way out of the hole.

"Sorry." He tried another smile, hoping to melt at least some of the ice. "My mouth got ahead of my brain."

"I'm sure it's happened a number of times before, Mr. Lassiter."

"It's Cam. Look, could we sit and talk like civilized people?"

"One of us can. I don't know what to expect from you, however." She settled herself in the chair.

Instead of taking the seat behind his mother's desk, he straddled the corner of her desk and faced his opponent, who still hadn't cracked a smile. "Why don't you tell me your impressions of Tio Johnson and his situation."

"Fine." She crossed her legs.

Cam tried not to stare.

"Tio's case is typical of so many I've seen."

"You've been working as a caseworker for..." He paused. "How many years?"

"Six. Since I graduated from Georgetown with a degree in psychology."

That caught him off guard. With that soft, almost breathy voice and wispy blond hair, she looked more like a college coed than a psych major who'd already worked for years in the field.

"As I was saying, Tio's case is typical. A father in prison, a mother who walked away from her responsibilities and an aged grandmother who is simply too old, too tired and too beaten down by the system to care for the boy.''

Cam grinned. ''That argument of age discrimination won't win you any points with most of the judges I've met.''

She flushed. ''You're right. I suppose I ought to temper my words, even though I honestly believe the grandmother in this case simply can't control an angry, hostile boy.''

''Don't blame it on age. My own grandfather is well past his prime and still cooks, cleans and is directly involved in all the Lassiter lives.''

''You have younger siblings?''

He shook his head. ''I'm the youngest.''

''You see? You and your siblings are raised. Furthermore, you have a mother who is educated and committed to her family.''

''Another bias showing, Ms. O'Connor. Education or the lack thereof should have no bearing on a person's ability to care for family. Furthermore, if you've looked into the juvenile system, you'll find that so many of the children entrusted to that institutional care fall through the cracks and become lost children. Is that what you want for Tio Johnson?''

''Don't twist my words, Mr. Lassiter. I want

what's best for my client. And right now, I feel that he would best be served in a juvenile facility until the courts determine his future.''

She had the most incredible green eyes, eyes that could go all soft or shoot sparks when he touched a nerve. It occurred to Cam that Summer O'Connor might look like a fragile flower, but she would certainly be a tough competitor.

Her voice went soft again, as though realizing that others in the outer office might overhear. ''As I see it, the real culprit here is Tio's father. He has no right encouraging the boy to see him in prison, when his influence can only be negative.''

''On that we can both agree.'' Cam's tone hardened. ''I have no use for a cop killer.''

''If that's so, then I challenge you to visit Tio's father in prison and plead on behalf of his son. Ask him to order the boy to stay away. If he agrees, I may allow Tio to remain in his grandmother's care. If he refuses, I have no choice but to place the boy in safe custody, for his own good. He can't afford to miss any more classes.''

''Why can't you visit the father in prison?''

''I did.'' She sighed. ''When he learned that

I was Tio's caseworker and considering taking the boy away from his grandmother, he went into a rage.'' She shivered just thinking about her reaction to Alfonso Johnson. She'd been absolutely terrified by the anger in him.

''Then what makes you think he'd see me?''

She looked him up and down, her lips curving for just the merest moment as she studied the expensive suit, the Italian leather shoes, the elegant designer watch at his wrist. ''You could hardly be mistaken for a social worker.''

He could have bristled at her remark. Instead he threw back his head and laughed. ''Yeah. I guess you're right.'' He thought a moment. ''But I have absolutely no interest in meeting this criminal.''

''Very well. I'll sign the documents today asking the judge to sever the grandmother's rights and demand that Tio go into a juvenile facility.''

His tone hardened. ''Why this rush to judgment?''

''Rush? Is that what you think? I suggest you read his file a little more closely. Tio has missed as much school this year as he has attended. If he misses any more days this year the school has the right to refuse him permission to return until he has made up all the material he missed or make him repeat the grade next year. Now, as this idiot social worker sees it, the boy's future is in the hands of a selfish father who wants to be an influence for evil in his son's life. If you find the thought of visiting a criminal in prison too offensive, don't blame the rest of us for the choices we make."

Cam could feel his temper, always carefully banked, beginning to heat. "If I agree to study his father's file, will you agree to hold off your decision for another day?"

She tapped a finger on the arm of the chair. "Another day takes us to the weekend. That means you're buying yourself some extra time, at the expense of my client."

"Not at the expense of, but on behalf of your client, Ms. O'Connor. I'm considering this only because I care about that boy."

"Then we've finally found common ground, Mr. Lassiter. Because I care about him, too." She considered, then nodded. "All right. I'll give you the weekend. But on Monday, my recommendations will go to the judge."

"As will mine." He took the file folder from

her hands and stared into those eyes. He'd thought them green. At the moment they were more gold than green. Cat's eyes. The thought made him smile. He'd better beware her claws. He had an idea he'd find them as sharp as her tongue.

"Until Monday, Ms. O'Connor."

He held the door and watched as she made her way through the outer office. Not only did she have great legs, but her backside wasn't bad either.

The thought had him grinning as his mother returned to her office. "Why the smile, Cameron?"

"Just enjoying the scenery." He turned and saw his mother's frown. "Sorry. I'm smiling because I've bought a little time. Summer O'Connor has just given me the weekend to study Alfonso Johnson's file." He held up the folder. "Is this all there is?"

His mother rummaged through her file drawer and came up with a bulging folder. "This is all I have. I'm sure the police and court files would be three times this size."

Cam gave a sigh, thinking about the golf game he'd hoped to fit in on the weekend. Now it looked as though he'd be spending his free time the way his mother spent hers.

"Homework," he muttered. "I always figured this ended when I got out of school. Now I seem to be doing more than ever."

"Join the crowd."

He started out of his mother's office, then on an impulse turned back. "What say we phone Pop and have him meet us for dinner downtown? The way he's been working lately, he'd probably enjoy a break."

Kate's smile was radiant. "That's a grand idea, Cameron." She picked up her cell phone and punched in the numbers, then waited.

"Kieran. Cameron is at my office. If you haven't started dinner yet, we thought you might enjoy meeting us downtown at..." She looked at her son questioningly.

Cam muttered, "Finnegan's."

"...at Finnegan's." She listened, then said, "Fine, Kieran. We'll see you there in an hour."

As she set aside the phone she laughed. "Knowing your grandfather, he'll be there first, to see that he gets the best booth."

"Not to mention time to sip a brew." Cam waited while his mother returned files to the drawer, clearing at least a little of the litter from her desktop.

"Come on." He dropped an arm around her shoulders. "I'll walk you to your car."

Kate couldn't help laughing as they stepped out the door. "I know you think this neighborhood is dangerous, but the people around here know me and look out for me."

He held her car door. "Yeah. Probably because you're the best thing that's ever happened to their neighborhood." He cleared his throat. "I know I don't say this often enough, but I'm really proud of the work you do."

Kate touched a hand to his cheek. "Thank you. And you make me proud, too, Cameron."

He closed the door, then walked to his car and followed his mother's lead into traffic.

His mind wasn't on his driving as he threaded his way between cars. He found himself smiling as he thought about Tio Johnson's caseworker, Summer O'Connor. He doubted that she would soon forgive or forget his slip of the tongue. Not that it mattered. If he could persuade her to change her mind and let the boy remain with his grandmother, they wouldn't have to see each other again.

Too bad, he thought. If they'd met under more favorable circumstances, it might have been fun to get to know her better.

Still, she wasn't his type. Too serious. He preferred to date women who were interested in a more laid-back, casual relationship.

He'd learned very early in life that there was no such thing as permanence. If his life should prove to be as fleeting as his father's, he intended to enjoy the hell out of it while he was here.

Chapter 3

Summer O'Connor parked her car at the North-side Apartments and collected her mail before taking the elevator to the sixth floor. Once inside her door she shed her shoes and tossed her purse and mail on a nearby table. Ignoring the blinking light on the phone machine, she headed toward the kitchen and poured herself a tall glass of ice water. Then she padded to the sofa and settled herself against the cushions, enjoying the silence.

There were days when she thought if she had to listen to one more voice whining about life's injustices, or one more supervisor complaining about lost paperwork, she'd simply walk away and never look back. Not that she ever would. The truth was, she loved her work. Loved knowing that she could make a difference in someone's life. Someone who might otherwise be lost.

If only she didn't have to deal with so many fools.

Like Cameron Lassiter.

She sighed and set aside the water. Everyone in the department knew about Kate Lassiter. How her husband, a decorated D.C. policeman, had taken the bullet meant for his partner, leaving a young widow with four children to raise alone. How Kate had gone back to school for her degree, and had earned the respect of everyone who knew her by turning her back on big money to work as a family advocate in the poorest section of the city.

Apparently her son didn't share her values. Everything about Cameron Lassiter screamed success and big bucks. The perfect haircut. The perfect suit. Even the perfect smile.

She'd had to work hard not to let that smile get to her. The first glimpse of him in the doorway with his mother had Summer's heart doing strange things. But then she'd overheard his sarcastic comment about Tio's idiot caseworker. She'd show him who the idiot was.

She knew all about guys like him. All flash and no substance. All they cared about was the way things looked. The flashy car parked outside the office could only belong to him. In a neighborhood like that, it was a wonder it hadn't been stripped. Of course, the people around there had too much respect for his mother to allow that. Still, it would have served him right, flaunting his possessions like a spoiled little rich boy in a neighborhood where people were barely getting by.

It wasn't that she disdained wealth. She'd grown up with it. Had even, in her youth, taken it for granted. But she'd met too many who enjoyed crowing about every success as though it made them somehow better than those less fortunate.

When the phone rang Summer ignored it and waited for the message machine to click on.

Her mother's voice broke through the stillness.

"Summer, where are you? I told you we were

celebrating your sister's birthday tonight before we leave for Europe. I hope the fact that you haven't answered means you're on your way. I told Rose to plan on serving dinner by half past seven."

Summer passed a hand over her eyes, feeling the beginning of a headache as she got to her feet and headed toward the shower.

The peace she'd been hoping for wasn't to be.

"Thanks for dinner, boyo." Kieran paused outside the Irish pub to clap a hand on his grandson's shoulder. "It was nice to take a night off."

"Yeah. I figured you were due for a break." Cam kissed his mother's cheek. "I'll see you both in the morning."

Kate arched a brow. "You aren't coming home with us?"

He shook his head. "If you don't mind, I'll spend the night in my old room. But I won't be there until late. I promised Elise Wentworth I'd stop by."

"I don't believe we've met her." Kate glanced at Kieran, who nodded his agreement.

"She's the niece of a client. It's not a romance."

Kieran grinned. "Would you like it to be?"

Cam shook his head. "There you go. Always scheming, aren't you, Pop? I've told you before. I'm not looking for a relationship. I much prefer a few laughs and no tearful goodbyes when it's time to move on."

"In other words, you haven't met the one yet?"

"The one?" Cam gave a roar of laughter. "Pop, I'm convinced there is no such thing as the one. I much prefer the woman of the moment to the woman of a lifetime."

"Spoken like a man who has never been in love."

Kate squeezed her son's hand. "Thanks for dinner, Cameron. I need to get home and do a little paperwork."

"See you tomorrow, boyo." Kieran turned away with a wink. "Don't do anything I wouldn't do."

"No need to worry. We won't be alone. Elise is expecting a houseful of company."

He climbed into his car and roared off down the street, heading toward Georgetown.

Cam had thought, once he arrived on this street of elegant mansions, he would have to check the addresses to find Elise's place. Instead, all he had to do was follow the crowd. There were so many cars arriving, a valet service had been hired to handle the parking.

He turned over the keys to his car and followed several couples up the wide stone steps lined with pots of ivy. Inside a maid was accepting wraps and directing the flow of people toward the main parlor.

Cam helped himself to a flute of champagne from a passing waiter and made small talk with several lawyers from his firm.

"Here you are." A pretty blonde took the champagne from his hand and sipped. "I told you to come for dinner."

Cam smiled. "Sorry. I was otherwise engaged."

She gave a mock pout. "I hope she was worth standing me up."

He let that pass without comment.

"Anyway, you're here now." She slipped her arm through his. "Come on. I'd like you to meet my parents."

Cam glanced around as they threaded their way through the crowd. "Nice place. Is it paid for?"

Elise giggled, and it occurred to Cam that she'd had more than a little champagne. "Did I tell you I'm leaving for Paris in the morning?"

"I don't believe you mentioned it. Is this job-related or a vacation?"

"Job?" She rolled her eyes. "Please don't say that in front of my father. He's been nagging me for months to find something useful to do. I think that's the only reason my mother is taking me out of the country. She figures if we spend enough time touring and shopping, Dad will miss us so much he'll forget to nag."

She paused before a cluster of people and touched a hand to the arm of a white-haired man who was laughing at someone's joke.

"Dad. You remember that nice young lawyer from Stern Hayes Wheatley that Uncle Don told you about? I invited him to my party."

The rest of the group turned to stare, and Cam caught sight of Summer O'Connor standing in their midst. He wondered if he looked as surprised as she did.

Before he could recover Elise said, "This is Cameron Lassiter. Cam, my father, Daniel O'Connor."

"O'Connor?" He accepted the man's handshake and glanced at Elise. "I thought your name was Wentworth."

"It is. That was the name of my husband. I kept it after the divorce." She caught hold of a woman's hand. "And this is my mother, Jeanine."

"Mrs. O'Connor."

Daniel O'Connor wrapped an arm around his older daughter, drawing her a little away from the others. "And this is Elise's sister, Summer."

Summer's tone was cool. "Mr. Lassiter and I have already met."

Elise looked from her sister to Cam. "You have? Well, isn't that interesting?" She put a proprietary hand over his, eager to get him away. "Uncle Don said to be certain to tell him the minute you got here, Cam. He's dying to talk business."

Cam hoped his annoyance didn't show. The last thing he wanted, after a meal of fish and chips and a hot fudge sundae, was to stand around at a boring party talking about a court battle he'd already waged and won.

He murmured the appropriate words of pleasure at meeting everyone before being led away by his hostess. Across the room he was forced to listen in polite silence while Elise's uncle replayed every highlight of a trial in which he'd been awarded one of the highest settlements in the district.

Nearly an hour later Cameron used a lull in the conversation to turn to Elise. "Sorry. I'm afraid I have to leave."

Her pout was more pronounced. "Since tomorrow is Saturday, you can't claim to have a morning court appearance. What could be more important than spending time with me? Especially since it's my last night in town."

He merely smiled. "There are half a dozen guys here drooling every time you move. The minute I leave you'll be so busy, you'll forget my name."

She started to walk with him to the door until she was stopped by one of the partners in Cam's firm.

Cam leaned close to whisper, "See? Told you." He brushed a kiss over her cheek and made his getaway while she was too busy to stop him.

When he stepped out the front door he found Summer on the steps waiting for her car.

She looked over. "Leaving so soon?"

He grinned. "Yeah. I've got this homework I agreed to do over the weekend."

"Poor baby. I'm sure it's going to get in the way of your fun."

"Not at all. I've always loved reading police rap sheets and delving into dysfunctional family histories."

His zany sense of humor was so unexpected, she burst into laughter.

Just then her car came to a stop at the foot of the steps, and the valet stepped out, holding her door.

As she settled herself inside Cam leaned in the window. "You ought to laugh more often, Summer."

She felt a little thrill along her spine and blamed it on the fact that he'd caught her by surprise. "Why?"

"You have a great laugh. It just…ripples."

"And you have a great line. In fact you probably have a million of them. All just rolling off your tongue like little pearls."

"Yeah. That's me. Smooth as champagne."

"I've noticed. That's why you and Elise make such a great pair. Speaking of my sister, I'm surprised she let you get away. She's usually more persuasive than that.'' Summer put her car in gear. ''Happy reading.''

As she drove away she watched his reflection in her rearview mirror. She'd give him this. He was certainly easy to look at.

But then, Elise had always had a fondness for rich, handsome jerks.

Cam was yawning as he opened the first file labeled Alfonso Johnson. After two glasses of champagne, he was moving like a slug. He promised himself he would only read the first few pages, then give in to the need to sleep.

Three hours later, the lights were still on in his old room as he read through hundreds of pages of Alfonso's files, beginning with the family court documents and continuing through police records of early arrests for break-ins and petty larceny. At age sixteen, he'd been convicted of robbing a neighborhood grocery store of beer and cigarettes. Two other minors were involved, but the court had charged all three as adults. After six months in jail, Alfonso had returned home and apparently had stayed clean for almost two years. Then at eighteen he was convicted of stealing a car and did time for that.

Back home, he married his childhood sweetheart, the mother of his three-year-old son, got
a job and appeared to have turned his life
around. Then when his son was five, he'd been
identified in a police lineup as the triggerman in
a robbery gone bad that ended with a police officer killed.

Cam rubbed his eyes and tossed the file aside.
He wasn't ready to read the details of the officer's death or the trial that followed. There may
be some who figured it was enough to know that
Alfonso Johnson would be doing hard time in
prison for the next twenty-five years of his life.
But at least he still had a life. What about the
police officer? What of his family? Had they
been blessed with a strong, loving mother? A
tireless, devoted grandfather? Had anyone been
there to help them over the rough spots?

He glanced at the bedside clock, annoyed that
he was wide awake at three in the morning.

He made his way downstairs to the kitchen.
Once inside he set the kettle on the stove and
walked to the big bay window to stare at the
faded basketball hoop.

"A little early for shooting hoops, isn't it,
boyo?"

At the sound of Kieran's voice he turned. "Yeah. I wouldn't want to wake the neighbors. What're you doing up, Pop?"

"I heard your footsteps. Thought I'd join you for a spot of tea." The old man glanced up when the kettle whistled. "I'll get the tea and pot, you get the cups."

The two worked together in companionable silence, making the tea, waiting while it steeped, then carrying it to the big trestle table, where they settled themselves.

"You've made your mother happy by agreeing to look into this boy's trouble." Kieran lifted the steaming cup to his lips and drank.

Cam stared into his cup. "The boy's caseworker, Summer O'Connor, is a piece of work."

"Summer, is it?" Kieran studied his grandson's frown. "I take it the two of you didn't hit it off."

"You might say that."

"What's the matter, boyo? Didn't she take to your Irish charm?"

"She was having none of it." He sipped his tea. "A funny thing. She was at the birthday party tonight in Georgetown. She turned out to be the older sister of Elise Wentworth."

"You don't say?" Kieran chuckled. "Does she approve of her little sister's boyfriend?"

"I'm not Elise's boyfriend. We're just friends. Her uncle was a client, and he introduced us. I think he was hoping we'd hit it off."

"And did you?"

Cam shook his head. "Elise isn't my type."

"Like her sister."

Cam's frown grew. "Funny. They don't seem at all alike. Elise is a party girl. She and her mother are leaving tomorrow for Paris. But Summer is all business."

"Dull, I suppose."

Cam sat back, considering. "Why would a woman who grew up in a mansion want to spend her days dealing with troubled kids from a ghetto?"

Kieran shrugged. "Why would a man working for one of the finest law firms in the city want to waste his time on helpless cases?"

"It's not a waste of time, Pop. So far we've had almost a dozen convictions overturned." The minute the words were out of his mouth, he turned to see his grandfather smiling. "Okay, I get your point, Pop."

Kieran's smile widened. "I'm sure it's the

same for this social worker. If she saves even one troubled kid, she'll feel that her time was well spent. It's what life's all about, boyo. We can work for money or we can work for the things that really matter.'' He drained his cup, then got up and crossed to the sink. ''I think I'll grab a little more sleep. You might want to do the same.''

''Yeah. Good night, Pop.''

When he was alone Cam sat brooding. He didn't know what annoyed him more. The fact that he had to spend the weekend finding a way to keep Tio Johnson with his grandmother, or the fact that he couldn't seem to get Summer O'Connor out of his mind.

Chapter 4

Summer settled herself at her desk and opened Tio's file. She'd spent the weekend reviewing all the information on his family background. The boy had been only five years old when his father was sent away to prison. His mother disappeared immediately after the trial, and the little boy's paternal grandmother, Willetta Johnson, petitioned for custody. She had been the only family member on either side to come forward and accept responsibility for the boy. After a brief background check, custody was granted.

The boy's early school records seemed normal

enough. He'd engaged in the usual fistfights on the playground. His grades had never been good, but at least they were passing until, at age ten, he'd begun a pattern of truancy that had escalated until this year, at age twelve, he had missed more classes than he'd attended. A representative from the school reported the truancy to the boy's grandmother, who was able to uncover the reason. The boy had been hitching rides to McCutchin Prison, nearly two hours from his home, to visit his father. Not only was he missing school, but he was putting himself in jeopardy by accepting rides with strangers.

Summer knew she was on solid ground by suggesting that the grandmother's custody be revoked. The woman had known about this problem for two years and had been unable, or unwilling, to solve it. She'd been given sufficient time, Summer thought, to change this dangerous behavior, if in fact she'd really wanted to.

If she couldn't control the boy, the juvenile system would.

Summer had arrived at her office half an hour earlier than usual just so she would be prepared for this Monday morning meeting with Cameron Lassiter.

Not a meeting, she corrected herself. It was a confrontation. And she'd do well to keep that in mind when he decided to pour on the charm.

He'd asked if they could use his mother's office, but Summer had refused. She had too much respect for Kate Lassiter to drag her into this. Unless she was mistaken, it could very well lead to a bloody, no-holds-barred battle of wills. There was no point in stacking the deck against herself by having Kate acting as intermediary.

Summer's office was as dingy as the others in the state-run agency. Peeling paint. Ugly metal desk. File cabinets that didn't close.

She didn't mind. She'd rather see the money go to the families they were trying to serve. Of course, she reminded herself, there was never enough money to go around. With public assistance, food stamps and a city-wide program to pay for heat during the winter, the people were still struggling just to make ends meet.

Still, she hadn't given up hope. If just one child got an education or just one family was able to hold together despite all the odds, it was a reason to celebrate.

Outside the dirty window overlooking the parking lot she saw the flash of a red car. A moment later she heard that deep-throated laughter and the answering sighs of the women in the outer office announcing the arrival of Cameron Lassiter.

When he paused in her doorway she felt an odd little flutter of her heart and told herself it was the rush of adrenaline, the anticipation of the coming battle.

She sat up straighter.

"Good morning." With his attaché case in one hand, he crossed the room and brought his other hand from behind his back, holding out a single red rose.

Summer had to struggle to keep the pleasure from her eyes. "Sorry. I don't keep any vases handy. We so rarely get flowers here at work."

"I know. That's why I brought this. Figured it would brighten your desk." He glanced around and spotted an empty cup from a gourmet coffee shop located in Georgetown. He studied the label. "Café latte. Good choice. This ought to do it." He stepped into the hallway and filled the cup with water from a cooler, then returned and set it in the middle of her desk.

She refused to look at it. Instead she folded her hands atop the open file folder. "I hope you found time from your busy social calendar to complete your weekend assignment.''

His grin was quick and deadly. "Yes, teacher.''

She sighed. The more he tried to be charming and funny, the more determined she was to keep this on a purely professional level. "I assume, after reading Alfonso Johnson's rap sheet, you're prepared to concede that he is the last person who should be influencing a troubled boy.''

Cam crossed one leg over the other, balancing the file folder on his lap as he began to thumb through the pages. "That was my first thought. According to these files, he appears to have graduated from petty larceny to grand larceny, and then to murder.''

She nodded, pleased and more than a little surprised at how quickly his attitude had changed. "Then you agree with me that it would be best to terminate Tio's grandmother's custody in favor of a juvenile facility.''

"Not at all.''

Her head came up. Cam could see the way her eyes went from cool to stormy.

"I see. You're one of those arrogant lawyers

who just has to win every argument, no matter what the cost to the other side.''

He merely smiled. "If you think that, Summer, you don't know me at all.''

Her voice chilled by degrees. "Nor do I care to.'' She snapped the file folder closed and shoved back her chair before standing. "I think this meeting is over. You didn't come here to be reasonable. You came here to teach Tio's idiot social worker a lesson.''

He took a moment to set his file aside before getting to his feet and coming around her desk. His voice was deceptively soft. "As I told you at the time, I'm sorry about that comment. It was said in a moment of stupidity.''

"I'm sure you have many such moments.''

His lips curved. "Yeah. Too many to count.''

His admission was unexpected.

He further caught her off guard by offering his hand. "I hope you'll accept my apology.''

She didn't want his apology. Nor did she want to shake his hand. But she felt backed into a corner. If she didn't at least make the attempt, she would appear unbending.

She placed her hand in his. A mistake. The heat that shot along her arm caught her completely by surprise. Instead of releasing her hand, he stepped closer. Just enough to have her backing up before she caught herself and stood her ground.

She looked up to find his eyes crinkled with unspoken laughter. That only caused her to lift her chin a fraction.

"I'm sorry to have wasted your time." She knew her voice sounded stiff and prim, but she was feeling far too intimidated by those laughing blue eyes and the way he stood here, invading her space without a trace of remorse.

"Any time I'm in the presence of a beautiful woman, it's hardly a waste of time."

"Your smooth lines are wearing thin." She withdrew her hand and started to turn away, then felt his hand at her shoulder.

She spun back, her eyes as cold as shards of ice. "I told you. This meeting is over."

"You didn't let me finish. I spoke with Warden Novicky about the fact that Alfonso Johnson's minor son was visiting without proper clearance. As you are well aware, a minor child must be accompanied by an adult when visiting a prisoner. It seems that a few of the guards are aware of it and willing to look the other way.

Not because Johnson is a model prisoner, you understand. Far from it. But they seem to feel that the visits are as good for the son as they are for the father.''

"I see." Her voice was pure ice. "Now we have prison guards acting as psychologists and bending the rules whenever it suits them."

Cam sighed. "I asked the warden to consider having Tio's name removed from the list of approved visitors. He said he would review the case and take it under advisement." He nodded toward the file on her desk. "Because the warden also had some interesting things to say about the importance of keeping contact between prisoners and their families, I've recorded our discussion for your perusal. I think when you've finished reading what he said, you'll agree with me that it is in both their interests to allow the boy to remain with his grandmother, and to visit his father as often as he can."

Summer was already shaking her head. "I can't believe what I'm hearing. Give me one good reason you changed your mind."

"According to the warden, Johnson is bitter, hostile and often considered just this side of dangerous. But he's a caring father. And probably the only hope Tio has of not finding himself in the same circumstances one day. If it's your job to help the kid find his way through this maze, Alfonso Johnson might be your best friend.''

"Or my worst nightmare." Summer swallowed. "I'll read your report. And then I'll make my recommendations."

"Thank you."

When he didn't move, she gave him a chilling look. "I'd like you to leave now."

"Yeah, I know. I can see that in your eyes." His smile was quick and dangerous. "How about what I'd like?"

"I don't care what you'd—"

The words died in her throat when he dipped his head and brushed her lips with his.

Her eyes went wide and stayed that way, fixed on his. She didn't blink. Didn't move.

Against her lips he murmured, "You're supposed to breathe."

She couldn't. Nor could she think. She supposed she ought to pull away. Act indignant. Slap his face. Instead, she stood, frozen in place, as the most amazing splinters of fire and ice danced through her veins.

He nuzzled her lips. She tasted like summer

rain. All cool and clean and fresh. With just a hint of tart lemon. The effect was startling.

Though he knew he'd overstepped his bounds, he couldn't step back. He found the combination of shock, outrage and gradual acquiescence in her unbelievably erotic. Beneath that cool facade he could taste the stirrings of passion. Hot. Sweet.

For the first time in ages he found himself wanting to forget all the rules and simply take and take until he was filled with this woman. For a moment the temptation was so great, he swayed against her, feeling the brush of her breasts in every part of his body.

He lifted his head and stared into her eyes, watching the way her vision seemed to blur, then focus, before narrowing on him with a fire that had him grinning.

She was surprised to find her hands clenched into fists at her sides. She could feel a tingling all the way to her fingertips. "As a lawyer you have to be aware that if I wanted, I could slap you with a harassment suit for that."

"Oh, yeah. I can see how much you resented this."

That had the heat rushing to her cheeks.

His tone softened. "I'm sorry if I offended you. But I'll be damned if I'll apologize for that kiss."

He took a step back, then picked up his file and started toward the door.

In the doorway he turned. "I left my cell phone number on the report so you can reach me when you've made your decision."

When he was gone Summer stood very still, dragging in several deep breaths before she sat down weakly in her chair.

She'd sounded like a pompous ass, accusing him of harassment. And all to cover her embarrassment at her lapse in judgment.

She drew in another ragged breath, then caught sight of the rose on her desk. It looked so silly here, in the midst of all this institutional dreariness.

She picked it up and inhaled the wonderful fragrance.

She turned toward the window just in time to see his snappy red car pulling into traffic.

For several seconds longer she stared into space, wondering at the way she had behaved when Cameron Lassiter had kissed her. Just thinking about him was having that same effect on her now.

She felt the way she did after swimming laps in her parents' pool. Heartbeat accelerated. Legs a bit shaky. Her breath coming hard and fast. Her brain high on adrenaline.

All that, and it had been little more than a whisper of a kiss. What would it be like if he ever decided to really pour himself into it?

Damn him for invading her thoughts like this. Even when he wasn't around, he was wasting her time.

Cam threaded his car through traffic. He needed to clear his mind in preparation for a meeting with the senior partners. They had a right to know what strategy he was planning to use in the coming trial. Even a firm as successful as Stern Hayes Wheatley didn't get the opportunity to aim for a billion-dollar windfall more than once or twice in a lifetime.

He was ready. The bigger the prize, the more calm and focused he became. He was certain that Summer O'Connor would call his attitude cocky or arrogant, but it was simply a fact.

Summer. What did he care what she thought?

But he did. And that bothered him more than he liked to admit.

What was he going to do about her? One minute he'd been ready to leave, the next he'd been kissing her. That kiss had been completely spontaneous. And what a kiss. It had rocked him to his soul.

It had been a long time since a woman had affected him like this. In fact, he couldn't remember the last time he'd been so rattled.

He'd like to think it was because this boy, Tio Johnson, meant so much to his mother. After all, Kate Lassiter had always been a sucker for a sad story, especially if it involved children. But he'd be lying if he tried to pin this on his mother or the kid. The truth had nothing to do with Tio Johnson and everything to do with Tio's gorgeous caseworker. There was just something about Summer O'Connor that had him baffled.

She might be easy to look at, but so were dozens of other women. She might have a bright mind that challenged him, but it wasn't her mind he'd been thinking about when he'd kissed her. In truth, once in her presence, his mind had been wiped clean of every thought but one. He'd wanted her. Desperately. And the feelings springing to life inside him hadn't been the least bit civilized. He'd felt, in that instant when their lips met, as primitive as a caveman. Doing the right thing, the proper thing, hadn't even entered the equation. He'd simply acted on impulse and to hell with the consequences.

He realized that, despite the fact that he'd cranked the car's air-conditioning as high as it would go, he was sweating. It had nothing to do with the weather, and everything to do with the woman who was playing with his mind.

He was in over his head and sinking quickly. And the worst part was, he didn't care.

He was going to see Summer O'Connor again.

And kiss her.

Of that he was absolutely certain.

Chapter 5

"Hi, Pop." Cam balanced his cell phone between ear and shoulder while he shrugged out of his suit jacket and tossed it over the passenger seat of his car.

"Where are you, boyo?"

"Stalled in traffic on the Beltway. An accident has cars backed up for miles. Who's coming for dinner tonight?"

"What makes you think anybody's coming over?"

"It's Friday night. You're making your pasta. Need I say more?"

Kieran laughed. "Well, Micah and Pru phoned to say they'd be here. And Donovan and Andi and the kids are driving down. I haven't heard from our Mary Brendan and Chris yet. But if they're free, I'm sure they'll stop by."

"Count me in. I don't know when I'll get there, but I'm bringing an appetite."

"Don't you always, boyo?" Kieran was still laughing as he rang off.

When his cell phone rang a few seconds later Cam picked it up. "Cam Lassiter here."

"Summer O'Connor." The voice was cool, controlled. "I finished my last case ahead of schedule and was able to return home early to read the details of your discussion with the warden regarding Alfonso Johnson."

Cam waited.

"Warden Novicky made some very valid arguments about the father remaining in contact with his son. But I'm afraid none of this changed my mind. I still believe an accused murderer will prove to be a harmful influence on a boy of Tio's age and temperament."

"I see." Cam paused and counted the number of silver cars he could see in the traffic jam. It was an anger-management method he'd learned from an instructor in high school. A way of distracting himself from an issue that might become explosive and have him speaking before thinking. "Have you had dinner yet?"

"Dinner?"

He could hear the confusion in Summer's voice. That had him smiling. "Yeah. You know. Food. Maybe a little wine. A quiet restaurant, off the beaten track."

"Sorry. After fighting traffic all day, nothing could persuade me to leave my place and deal with any more crazy drivers."

"All right. How about if I bring dinner to you?"

"I don't think..."

He caught sight of an advertisement for an Italian restaurant less than a block from where he was sitting. "Pasta drenched in sauce. Breadsticks with just a hint of garlic."

He heard her sigh and decided to press his advantage. "I can be in Georgetown in half an hour."

She laughed. "That's nice, but I'm afraid it won't do me any good. I live at the Northside Apartments in Silver Spring."

"The Northside? I had a law school friend

who lived there." He calculated the time. "Give me an hour. What's your number?"

"Six thirty-one. On the sixth floor."

"See you in an hour." He rang off, then phoned his grandfather. "Pop? I'm afraid I won't be able to make dinner. Tell Micah he can have my share."

Kieran laughed. "It's your loss, boyo. Where are you headed?"

"Got a date with a cool blonde." Just thinking about her had Cam reaching over to turn on the air-conditioning and raise the car windows before rolling the sleeves of his monogrammed shirt. It was a typically steamy June afternoon, but until now he hadn't been at all offended by the heat and the exhaust fumes.

Whistling a tune, he used the nearest exit to escape the traffic.

Summer stared at the phone in her hand wondering how this had happened. One minute she was preparing herself for an argument and the next she was agreeing to dinner with Cameron Lassiter.

And not just dinner anywhere. Right here in her apartment.

What had she been thinking? Once again she'd been robbed of her common sense. And all because of one very slick con artist.

No wonder he was so passionate about defending Alfonso Johnson. They were probably soul mates. The only difference between those two men was that one was at the mercy of the law and the other practiced it.

She started toward her bedroom, stripping off her work clothes as she walked. After a cool shower she'd be prepared to face the enemy on her own turf.

Cam shifted carryout bags to one hand and punched in the button to Summer's apartment. Seconds later a buzzer sounded, and he pushed open the main door before heading toward the elevator.

On the sixth floor he followed the arrows and felt a moment's confusion when he caught sight of Summer standing in the open doorway to her apartment. He'd been picturing her in a prim business suit. Instead she was wearing some sort of soft, clingy slacks and a pale pink shirt that seemed to hug every line and curve of her body. Her hair was still damp from the shower and had been brushed long and loose, spilling around her face in a cloud of soft waves.

She couldn't help laughing at the jumble of bags. "Did you invite an army to join us?"

He grinned. "I don't know about you, but I'm starving."

He stepped past her and breathed her in. She smelled like a field of wildflowers.

He glanced around as she closed the door. "Nice place."

"Thanks." She led the way to the small kitchen. "I looked at a few houses in the area, then talked myself out of them. There just isn't time in my life to take care of a house."

"I know what you mean." He set the bags on the island counter, then began removing cartons. It pleased him to note the single red rose on her countertop. She'd taken it out of the paper cup and placed it in a tiny crystal bud vase. "I bought a place nearly a year ago, and I'm still spending more nights in my old room at my mother's place than I am in my own home." He glanced around. "I'll need a skillet for this chicken cacciatore."

"I thought you promised me pasta."

"I did. And you'll have some. But I got carried away with all the other choices offered."

Intrigued, Summer handed him a heavy skillet and watched as he dumped the contents of a carton into it before setting it on the stove.

He held up a bottle of Chianti. "I hope you have a corkscrew."

She rummaged in a drawer and found one. While he opened the wine she set two stem glasses on the counter.

He poured and handed one to her, enjoying the swift rush of heat as their fingers brushed. From the way her eyes narrowed, she'd felt it, too.

"Here's to the end of the work week."

"For you, maybe. I'll be reading reports all weekend."

"Yeah." He smiled, watching the way she backed up when he leaned too close. "Too bad we have to work for a living."

He turned to lower the heat and stir the contents of the skillet.

Summer leaned a hip against the counter. "You look like you know what you're doing."

"Do I?" He shot her a smile. "I've been helping Pop in the kitchen since I was five."

"Pop?"

"My grandfather. He lives with us and pretty much does everything around the house. He's the cook, shopper, cleaner. And all-around boss."

"That must be nice for your mother."

"Yeah. It frees her up to do her thing." He looked around. "Got a platter?"

"Up here." She reached into a cupboard over the stove. When she turned she found herself brushing his body. She was aware of the little curls of pleasure along her spine. "Will this do?"

"Yeah." The smile on his face had her backing up. "That's perfect."

"Well, I..." She felt the wine slosh over the rim of her glass and set it down quickly. "Guess I'd better set the table."

"Good idea." Cam waited until she walked to the little glass-topped table. With the counter between them he could breathe again. He picked up his glass and drank, needing something for his parched throat. This wasn't going to be as easy as he'd thought. The minute he got too close to Summer O'Connor, all the energy left his brain and seemed to flow to another part of his anatomy.

"What's in this bag?" Summer crossed to the counter.

"Cheese rolls. Antipasto. And salad for two."

She began dividing the salad into two pretty crystal bowls. "If you ask me, there's enough here for two dozen."

He laughed. "This is the first time I've fed you. I didn't know if you had an appetite like a bird or like King Kong."

"Judging by all this food, I know what kind yours is."

"Yeah. Thanks to Pop, the Lassiters all have an appreciation for fine food." He added two small side dishes of pasta and began carrying everything to the table.

Summer was laughing as she took her seat. "If you and I manage to eat all this food, we'll be too full to get up from the table."

"That's the plan. I figure you'll be a captive audience while I expound on my theory that Alfonso Johnson could actually be a role model for his son, Tio."

"Dream on." She shook her head while he topped off their wineglasses. "I don't think even your silver tongue will manage to persuade me of that.'' She took her first taste of chicken and sighed. "Oh, this was definitely worth waiting for.''

"Good. I'm glad you approve.'' He followed suit and was pleasantly surprised. He'd chosen the carryout restaurant at random and was afraid he'd be disappointed. That was one reason he'd brought so much food. If the first course failed, he'd intended to salvage it with a second choice, or even a third.

He tasted the pasta and nodded. "Not as good as Pop's, but close.''

"Your grandfather's a good cook?''

"The best. Especially his pasta. Whenever we know he's fixing it, the entire family shows up for dinner.''

"I suppose it's an easy way to impress your dates.''

He shrugged. "I wouldn't know. I've never brought any of them home to sample Pop's pasta.''

She arched a brow. "Not even Elise?''

Cam studied her over the rim of his glass. "I never actually had a date with Elise.''

"What's that supposed to mean?''

"It means that your uncle was jubilant after his court case was won and impressed by the brash young lawyer who saved his hide."

"That brash young lawyer being you?"

He grinned. "Your uncle did his best to bring your sister and me together. It was at his insistence that I attended her birthday celebration. But we never went out on a date."

"I'm sure you can correct that oversight when she gets back from Europe."

He shook his head. His voice, usually so smooth, held the thin edge of steel. "It's not going to happen. Especially now."

At her questioning look he merely smiled and passed the rolls. "If you don't hurry up and eat, I'll beat you to all the good stuff."

Summer dug into her food, amazed at the improvement to her appetite. It wasn't the knowledge that he hadn't dated Elise, she told herself. But a small voice inside her mind was telling her that it did matter. It mattered very much. If there had been anything at all between this man and someone she loved, she would immediately back off.

Cam helped himself to more chicken cacciatore. "Tell me about your family."

She broke a roll and buttered it. "My father and mother owned the Westcourt Galleries until a year ago, when they sold the company to an international conglomerate."

Cam paused. No wonder the house in Georgetown had been filled with such impressive art and artifacts. "I've seen those galleries in my travels."

Summer nodded. "Besides the one here in Washington, they have branches in New York and Paris and London. My parents had always hoped Elise and I would follow them into the business, but it had no appeal to us, so they finally accepted an offer to sell."

"Are they enjoying retirement?"

She laughed. "They don't know the meaning of the word. My father is considering accepting an appointment as ambassador to Ireland. My mother still acts as buyer for the galleries."

"So this trip to Europe is strictly business?"

Summer considered. "A little business, a little pleasure. Like Mother, Elise enjoys the shopping. The two of them will have a grand time buying out Europe."

"How about you?" Cam dug into his salad. "Why didn't you go along?"

She shook her head. "After a day or two I'd go stark raving mad. I've never been able to spend long days doing nothing more challenging than finding a bargain."

"But with a background like yours, why social work?"

"I guess it comes naturally to me. My father said, in all our travels, I was always standing up for the underdog. At any rate, I knew from the time I started college that I wanted to do something that would make a difference." She sat back, surprised to find her plate empty. "What about you? Why law?"

He shrugged. "I thought about following my older brothers into government service. Micah was a Secret Service agent. Donovan..." He grinned. "Donovan never talks about his work, so we assume it was some kind of top-secret stuff like CIA. But I found myself intrigued with my mother's law classes. After my degree, I interned with Stern Hayes Wheatley, and they asked me to stay on."

"Considering their reputation, you must be good."

"Careful. Any minute now you might forget I'm the enemy and say nice things about me."

There was that smile again. Quick enough and dangerous enough to have her heart reacting in the strangest way. "Oh, I doubt I'll go that far." She indicated the empty platters. "But I will admit that you have excellent taste in carryout. And Italian food is a real weakness of mine."

"Any other weaknesses I ought to know about?"

"Chocolate." She laughed and pushed away from the table, returning with two cups of steaming coffee.

"I'll remember that for next time."

She picked up her cup. "What makes you think there'll be a next time?"

He sipped, then met her look across the table. "Maybe you won't be able to resist my charm."

"Right. And maybe pigs fly."

That had him chuckling. He surprised her by starting to clear the table.

"You don't have to do that. You brought the food. The least I can do is clean up."

"If we do it together it'll be done in half the time." While she carried the rest of the dishes, he loaded the dishwasher.

When the table was cleared she topped off their cups and led the way to the great room.

They settled into comfortable overstuffed chairs with a small, round table between them. When Cam merely sat back and said nothing, Summer glanced at him with a look of suspicion.

"Isn't this the time when you try to convince me to allow Tio to continue to visit his father in prison?"

Cam merely shrugged. "You said my discussion with the warden hadn't changed your mind."

"That's right. But I thought the whole purpose of your visit was to try again."

"Is that what you thought?" He sipped his coffee.

Intrigued, she tucked her legs under her and watched him. He looked entirely too smug. "What are you up to?"

"You have a very suspicious mind, Ms. O'Connor."

"When a man plies me with food and wine, I figure he wants something in return."

"My, my. I can see that you've been hanging around with the wrong kind of men." He drained his cup and got to his feet. "It's time for me to say good-night."

"Good-night?" She set her half-filled cup on

the table and followed him to the door of her apartment. ''Well, thank you for this lovely surprise.''

''You're welcome.''

He opened the door and stepped out.

''Cam.'' Puzzled, Summer paused in the open doorway and touched a hand to his shoulder.

He turned. ''Something I forgot?''

''No. I just wanted…'' She felt her face flame. In truth, she'd expected him to kiss her again. Had wanted him to. ''If you'd like, I'll read your report again. Maybe I was a bit hasty.''

He shrugged. ''Whatever you'd like, Summer.''

She cleared her throat. ''I'll call you tomorrow.''

''I won't be home. I promised Tio that if he didn't miss any school this week, I'd drive him to prison to visit with his father.''

''You what?''

''I said I…''

She lifted her hand, palm up, cutting him off. ''I heard you. I can't believe you would go behind my back like this.''

Instead of the argument she anticipated, he merely leaned close and gave her a devilish smile. "I love what happens to your eyes when you get mad."

"Don't try that phony charm." She started to pull back, but he snagged her wrist and held her close.

"They could cut out a man's heart at twenty paces. And when you're aroused, they could melt glaciers." He leaned even closer, until she could feel the warmth of his breath on her cheek. "I had every intention of leaving without tempting myself." His smile was deceptive. "But now I believe I'm going to have to kiss you."

Before she could frame a refusal he cupped a hand to the back of her head and covered her mouth with his.

She experienced the most incredible heat racing through her veins until she was staggered by it. She felt the room do a slow tilt that caused her to reach out and clutch blindly at his waist.

His lips were warm and firm and agile, moving over hers with a skill that had the breath backing up in her lungs. With nothing more than his mouth on hers, he had her heart tumbling in her chest and her mind taking her to the most dangerous places. The thought of lying in his arms, his hands on her, had the blood throbbing in her temples. She couldn't resist the little purr of pleasure that escaped her lips.

When he finally lifted his head, he stared at her and touched a hand lightly to her cheek. "I don't know about you, but to my way of thinking that was better than chocolate."

He strode down the hall, leaving her staring silently after him. Hoping the floor would soon stop swaying.

Chapter 6

Summer stood on the little balcony off the kitchen, watching a spectacular sunrise. Thanks to Cameron Lassiter, she'd put in a less than restful night.

He'd caught her off guard. After so many psych classes, she thought herself an excellent judge of character. But Cam refused to fit neatly into any slot. She'd scorned him for being just another hotshot lawyer trying to make a name for himself. It was true that he was bright enough and ambitious enough to be employed by one of the finest law firms in a city filled with outstanding legal minds. Why then was he taking a day off to drive an inner-city kid to visit a prison inmate? Was he just doing this to irritate her? Or was there something more going on here?

She sipped her coffee and thought about all the contradictions in this man. He was smooth and glib and, from her own observations, very sure of himself with women. Yet last night he'd been laid-back and fun. She had to admit that she'd had a really good time. Of course, if she wanted to be completely honest, she would also have to admit that she was greatly relieved to learn that there had been nothing between Cam and her sister. Especially after that kiss. She couldn't remember when she'd been so affected by a simple kiss. Yet he'd apparently had every intention of leaving without kissing her. In truth, she'd been the one to call him back. She couldn't even recall why, though if she wanted to be honest with herself, it was because she'd been puzzled by his lack of interest.

And then that kiss.

Had it all been an act? Had he pretended indifference just to gauge her reaction? Or had that kiss been purely spontaneous?

Either way, the effect had been devastating. He'd cost her a night's sleep. Even now, miles away, he was messing with her mind.

She set the empty cup aside and leaned on the balcony railing. Maybe, after a long shower, she would read Cam's report again, and withhold her decision. At least until he reported on Tio's visit with his father.

After submitting to a search for weapons and contraband and filling out the proper forms, Cam sat in the dingy room at McCutchin Prison and watched as Tio Johnson signed the visitor's log and was handed a pass. By now Cam was used to the drill. But he could still recall his shocking introduction to the impersonal treatment meted out to those who came to visit prisoners.

Many of the people who came here to visit friends and relatives had driven for hours. Yet once they arrived, they found little hospitality. No vending machines offering food or drink. No soft chairs to ease old, tired bones. Not a shred of comfort afforded those who waited in the crowded, airless room, sometimes for hours.

His first glimpse of a state prison had occurred when, as a novice lawyer at Stern Hayes Wheatley, he'd agreed to a request by his mother to look into the conviction of a gang member doing twenty years for murder. He smiled, remembering. He hadn't wanted to get involved. His work at the firm was heady stuff for a young lawyer. He'd found himself dealing with international financiers, politicians, global movers and shakers. He was already spending fifty and sixty hours a week struggling to keep up with the workload. But as a favor to his mother he had agreed to read the file.

It had been a shocking discovery. Though it had taken a little digging, Cam had uncovered glaring flaws in the case. When confronted, the court-appointed lawyer who'd handled the defense had admitted that he'd had little time to prepare a case. After only two days of testimony a jury had convicted, and a judge had been forced to follow the letter of the law and sentence the convicted man to twenty years.

It still gave Cam a thrill to realize that it was his hard work that had uncovered enough questions to force a new trial. What had started out as a favor to Kate Lassiter had ended with an innocent man being reunited with his family.

For a lawyer who spent all his time in court

battling for money for his already wealthy clients, it was heady stuff indeed to gain a man's freedom. To be instrumental in giving him back his life.

It had been the beginning of a secondary career that was starting to take up as much of his time as his primary employer. Still, he couldn't bring himself to stop. Each time he helped free an innocent man, Cam found himself a little more eager to take on the challenge again.

Still, this one was different. Alfonso Johnson's crime was a little too close for comfort. Though Cam hadn't had time to review the trial transcripts, he had formed an instant dislike for the man in light of what he'd done. The only reason Cam had come today was to keep his word to the man's son.

The boy took his seat beside Cam. They had driven for nearly two hours from the city in total silence.

The boy was small and wiry and looked lost in the faded baggy denims and dingy T-shirt. His sneakers had so many holes in them, they were barely holding together. But it wasn't his clothes that set him apart; it was his anger. He wore it like a badge.

"What time did they assign you?"

The boy didn't bother to look at Cam. "Noon."

Cam studied the pass in the boy's hand, then caught sight of the bruised knuckles. "Looks like you use your fists. You any good?"

Tio shrugged. "When I have to be."

"How often is that?"

The boy's head came up. Heat flared briefly in his eyes. "Whenever anybody says something about my dad doing time."

"You get teased about him?"

He looked down at his shoes. "Yeah."

"How're you doing in school?"

"Fine."

"That's not what I heard."

The slender shoulders moved. "I'm failing. Big deal."

"It'll be a big deal one day."

"Yeah? When?"

"When you're too big for school and can't get a job. When your grandmother's dead and your father's still in the joint and you're out on the street."

"I can take care of myself." To escape, Tio

lurched out of his seat and leaned against the far wall, arms crossed over his chest.

Annoyed with himself, Cam leaned back and stretched out his long legs, trying to find a comfortable position on the hard metal chair.

Good going, Lassiter. I'm sure that'll straighten the kid out. Now why don't you go over there and kick him while he's down?

He pulled a bag of peanuts out of his pocket and decided to try again. Crossing the room he held it out. "Have some."

His offer was greeted with stony silence.

He popped a handful into his mouth, then held out the bag. "You need these."

"What for?"

"To fuel that temper. Did you know that anger burns twice the calories of laughter?"

"Says who?"

"I read it in a comic book."

That had the boy looking at him.

"Okay. So maybe it was a textbook. But when I was your age, I got a lot of my information out of comic books. You read any good ones lately?"

Tio didn't smile. But he did reach for the bag

of peanuts and fill his hand before giving it back. "I hate reading."

"That's your first mistake. Reading is your way out."

"Out of what?"

"This life you're so fond of."

The boy gave him a long, steady look. "You think you're smart."

"I am. And you know how I got that way?"

Tio didn't respond.

"By reading. If you can read, you can teach yourself anything." Seeing that the boy wasn't going to speak to him, he held out the bag.

The two stood munching in silence until a guard shouted, "Johnson. Tio."

The boy hurried forward, then waited until a second guard led him through an open doorway into the visitor's section. Cam crumpled the bag and stuffed it into his pocket before taking a seat. It was going to be a long day.

Cam threaded the car through traffic while the boy sat, sullen and silent, in the passenger seat. The angry, nervous tap of his foot was the only sign of his agitation.

Spotting a diner, Cam looked over. "I don't know about you, but I'm starving."

In the parking lot he turned off the ignition and pocketed the keys. "Come on. I'll buy you some lunch."

Tio followed him inside where they found an empty booth. A young woman in shorts and a T-shirt came for their order.

Cam glanced at Tio. "How about a burger and fries?"

When the boy nodded he turned to the waitress. "Two burgers and fries and two tall root beers."

When their order came Tio wolfed his down without even tasting it.

Cam polished off a fry. "How about another?"

The boy shook his head. "Gram will have supper waiting."

"You like living with your grandmother?"

Tio shrugged. "It's okay. I'd rather be with my dad."

"We can't always have what we want."

Tio's nostrils flared. "Who said anything about 'we'? Looks like you got everything you want. Big flashy car." He nodded toward the gold watch on Cam's wrist. "You didn't buy that in no pawnshop."

Cam grinned. "You got that right. I came by all this the old-fashioned way. By working hard."

The boy studied him. "Those hands are too soft for hard work. My dad worked from morning until dark every night. He was the strongest dad in the neighborhood. I can still remember the way he could carry me and three friends in his arms with room to spare."

"That's strong." Cam smiled. "What did your father do?"

"He hauled other people's garbage. It was the only work he could get." Tio's voice lowered. "But it wasn't good enough for some people."

This was, Cam realized, the closest the boy had ever come to mentioning his mother. He deliberately kept his tone gentle. "Some people want more than they have."

"Nothing ever satisfies some people." The boy's eyes flashed. "Give 'em the moon, they'll ask for the stars. That's what my dad says."

"What does your dad want?"

"His life back. My dad told me today that if he ever got another chance, he'd never complain again about hauling garbage."

Cam fell silent, thinking about the man Alfonso Johnson was accused of killing. Dead men didn't get second chances.

Aloud he merely said, "I guess the life that seemed pretty dreary can look awfully good once it's been taken away." Seeing the waitress heading toward them he dug in his pocket and handed her some money before leading the way out to the car.

As they rejoined the streams of traffic Cam glanced at the boy beside him. "I knew a kid who thought he was pretty good with his fists. Used to pick fights with guys twice his size just for the fun of it."

That had Tio's interest. "Did he get his butt kicked?"

Cam nodded. "A lot. That just made him madder and tougher. So he picked more fights. He got kicked out of so many schools, there weren't any left that would consider taking him. Except one. Military school."

"Wow." The boy shook his head from side to side. "Now that's one unlucky dude."

"Yeah. He wasn't happy. But he had no choices left."

"What'd he do?"

Cam sighed. "He had to find other outlets for his anger."

"How?"

"By becoming the kid everybody else had to beat in class. He stayed up studying half the night, hiding a flashlight under the blankets, just so he'd get the highest grade on a test."

Tio snorted. "What was that supposed to prove?"

"That he could leave everyone in his dust."

The boy looked unimpressed. "I suppose you're going to tell me he grew up to be President or something."

"Nope." Cam brought his car to the curb outside the tired-looking old house Tio shared with his grandmother. "But he took some satisfaction out of graduating at the top of his class. And he found out that there are all kinds of ways to fight and win."

The boy opened the car door and climbed out. Once on the sidewalk he turned and called through the open window, "I'd still rather fight with my fists."

"Yeah." Cam smiled. "There's something to be said for the crunch of fist against bone. Unless—" his smile faded "—the other guy has a

gun. Then you might find yourself wishing
you'd challenged your opponent to a battle of
brains instead of brawn.'' He lifted a hand in
salute. ''If your grandmother tells me you stayed
in school all week, I'll see you again next weekend for another visit with your dad. Deal?''

The boy considered, then nodded glumly.
''Deal.''

It occurred to Cam as he pulled away that Tio
Johnson wasn't nearly as upset about their agreement as he let on. The kid may want to spend
more time with his father, but he was smart
enough to know that he could have the best of
both worlds by faithfully going to class all week,
then enjoying a free ride to prison on the week-
ends.

It solved the boy's problem.

Cam's was another one altogether. In order to
keep Tio out of the juvenile system, he was going to have to get busy on Alfonso Johnson's
court transcript.

He couldn't think of a more unpleasant task
than revisiting the trial of a convicted cop killer.

Chapter 7

Summer snatched up the phone before the second ring. Hearing Cam's voice, her own softened. "How did Tio's visit go with his father?"

"I wouldn't know. He didn't bother to give me a blow-by-blow."

"He must have said something."

"Not a thing. But I offered to drive him to prison again next weekend if he promised to stay in school all week. That is, if he's still living with his grandmother a week from now."

"Did Tio agree?"

Cam sighed. "Not in so many words, but I

have a feeling he'll give it a try. Why not? Being picked up and delivered in my car beats standing in the heat hitching rides with strangers."

She could hear the weariness in his tone and without considering the implications blurted, "Do you have plans for dinner?"

He paused just a beat before saying, "No. How about you?"

"I thought I'd grill some chicken. Want to join me?"

"I've never turned down a home-cooked meal in my life. What time?"

"How about now?"

His day just turned from gray to golden. "I'm on my way."

Cam sprinted from his car to the main door of the apartment complex and rang the buzzer. It was amazing how quickly his weariness had fled at the thought of spending the evening with Summer.

Minutes later he stepped out of the elevator on the sixth floor and hurried along the cool hallway. Before he could knock the door was opened.

Summer was wearing one of those long, ankle-skimming sundresses the color of raspberry sherbet. She'd pulled her hair up in a knot with little tendrils kissing her cheeks. On her feet were strappy sandals.

She glanced at the handled bag, bearing the logo of one of the area's finest gourmet shops. ''Wine?''

''Champagne. I thought the day called for something special.'' He stepped past her.

When she turned, he had to stop and swallow. There was almost no back to the dress. All that cool, pale skin robbed him of breath.

''The chicken's on the grill.'' She pointed to the little balcony before opening a cupboard door to search for champagne flutes.

He crowded in beside her and began fiddling with the cork. Though the air was on and her apartment cool, he was sweating. He popped the cork and watched as the champagne frothed. Then he filled two flutes and handed one to her.

She smiled at him. ''What will we drink to?''

His eyes met hers. ''Too cool blondes in backless dresses.''

She could feel her cheeks redden even while she laughed. ''I debated changing into something else.''

"I'm glad you didn't." He was grateful for the icy liquid that slid down his parched throat. "If you'd rather, we can drink to chocolate." He opened the bag to reveal a lavish foil box.

"You remembered."

"How could I forget your weakness?" He could see her debating whether to indulge herself or wait. "Go ahead. Have one."

She laughed again. Quick. Musical. "I didn't realize I was that transparent." She shook her head. "It'll spoil my appetite."

"Haven't you heard?" He held out the box, daring her. "Chocolate actually stimulates the appetite."

"You're making that up."

"Maybe." He popped a chocolate maple cream into his mouth and sighed. "But it works for me."

"All right." She followed suit. On a sigh she closed her eyes. "Oh, double chocolate fudge." She nodded. "You're right. Now I'm starving."

As she squeezed past him, she was aware of the way her body strained toward his.

She slid open the glass door leading to the balcony. "I'd better turn that chicken."

Cam stood a moment alone in the kitchen.

Had he imagined the sizzle between them just now?

Needing something to do, he rummaged through the cupboards until he located a deep crystal bowl. He filled it with ice, picked up the champagne and chocolate and stepped out.

When he looked around he was pleasantly surprised. Besides a small wrought-iron table and two chairs, there were pretty pots filled with a glorious array of flowers in pinks and whites and purples. In one corner of the balcony was a fountain, a smooth column of marble over which spilled a cascade of water. The sound of it, mixed with the perfume of flowers and the cool shade of the building, made for a lovely, relaxing bit of paradise.

"This is great."

Summer looked up from the grill. "I love this spot. It's the next best thing to having a yard."

He tucked the champagne on ice, then took a turn around the balcony, admiring the work that had gone into it. "With this much talent, you really ought to have a house and yard."

"I'm inclined to agree with you." She opened a foil pouch of vegetables, releasing fragrant steam. "There's just one problem. I have this job that seems to take up way too much of my time.''

"I know the feeling." His voice, so close behind her, had her looking over her shoulder. "Need some help?"

She shook her head.

"Then let me fill that glass." He took the flute from her hand.

When he walked away Summer reminded herself to breathe in and out. It wasn't easy when he was so close his warm breath tickled the nape of her neck.

Seconds later he returned. The heat seemed to follow him.

She sipped, grateful for the cool slide of liquid velvet. "Tell me about your day with Tio."

"Not much to tell. We didn't exchange too many words. I gave him a lecture on learning to use his brain instead of his fists. I came off sounding like a fool. After his visit with his father, I bought him lunch. Then, to make up for being such a jerk I told him I'd offer him the same deal next weekend, if he stayed in school." Cam's hand fisted atop the balcony railing. "That's pretty much it."

Summer closed a hand over his. "Why are you beating yourself up over this?"

"Because I don't know how to reach him."

"At least you're trying, Cam. That's more than most people are willing to do."

He shook his head. "Look. I'm not even sure how much I care about the kid. I'm in this because my mother asked me for a favor. I've always thought I could do anything for her. But she wants me to look at Alfonso's transcript and see if there's a chance for a retrial. I'm not sure I can do that."

Summer nodded in understanding. "Because he's convicted of killing a police officer."

"Yeah. I don't think I can get beyond that."

Summer sipped her champagne as she digested this information. "How do you think your mother is able to get beyond it?"

Cam shrugged. "She's just a much better person than I am. She's always had this amazing ability to work through her pain."

"What did you do to get through the pain of losing your father?"

He looked away. "I did a lot of fighting."

"A tough guy, huh?"

"Yeah." His smile crept back as he turned to

her. "I developed a mean left hook. And then I was persuaded to develop my brain instead."

"I'd say it worked."

His laughter warmed. "I don't know. There's something satisfying about rattling a few bones. I've always enjoyed a good knock-down-drag-out fight. But in the long run it's a lot easier practicing law than trading punches. And the pay's better."

Relieved to see his sense of humor return, Summer began filling a platter. "Come on. That chocolate gave me a big appetite."

"I told you so." He tugged on a strand of her hair, sending heat straight to her core.

When he walked to the little table, she had to take a moment to catch her breath. Then she followed him, setting the platter down before taking the chair he was holding.

"Did you meet Tio's grandmother?" Summer spooned wild rice onto her plate, then passed the rice to Cam.

"Yeah. She seems like a nice lady, trying to cope with a son in prison and an angry grandson who keeps testing her patience." He helped himself to the rice, then added chicken and vegetables before holding the platter while Summer did the same.

"Does she seem overwhelmed having a grandson living with her?"

Cam buttered a roll warm from the grill. "Not that I noticed. In fact she said having Tio with her eased her loneliness."

Summer winced.

Seeing it, Cam reached across the table to lay a hand over hers. "Now who's beating herself up?"

"I'm the one who wants to take Tio away from her, remember?"

"Only if you decide it's the right thing to do. As I recall, you're still weighing your options."

She sighed. "Only because a certain persuasive lawyer has been working his charm on me."

"Really?" He looked enormously pleased with himself. "You mean I'm the only reason you haven't made a decision?"

"As if you didn't know." She was relieved when he lifted his hand. Her own was none too steady as she picked up her fork and started to eat.

He tasted. Smiled. "This is good."

"Thanks. I make it a lot, when I'm too tired

to eat out. It's so simple. I just throw everything on the grill, and by the time I've showered and changed into something comfortable, it's ready.'' She sipped her champagne. ''How about you? Do you prefer eating at home or eating out?''

''I do a little of both. But home is definitely better.''

''Really? Why?''

He couldn't stop the smile that curved his mouth. ''You'd have to meet my family. They're noisy and bossy, and when we get together for dinner, which is at least once or twice a week, it's a party. Pop calls the tune, and the rest of us dance to it.''

''Sounds like you have a fascinating family.'' She sat back, a pensive look crossing her face. ''I think it would be fun to have siblings that you enjoy as friends.''

He studied her. ''I take it you and Elise aren't exactly close.''

She sighed. ''We never were. Even as children. I think we've reconciled ourselves to the fact that we'll never travel in the same circle.'' She brightened. ''My dad called earlier. We're having dinner tomorrow night, before he flies out to Ireland.''

"It sounds like you count him among your friends."

She nodded. ''We have a special relationship. I've always known that I could go to him with any problem. From the time I was very young, I've always been comfortable telling him whatever was on my mind.''

"That's nice." Cam studied her across the table. "I've always thought that's the way it would have been for me with my dad."

"Do you remember him?"

He frowned, and for a moment she thought he might not answer. Then he shrugged. ''The truth is, I'm not sure what I remember and what I've heard so often that I only think I remember.''

"I don't understand."

"At first, we all grieved in silence. Maybe it was too deep for words." He shrugged. ''Anyway, after a while my family decided to keep Riordan Lassiter alive, at least in our own home. To that end my grandfather, my mother, my sister and brothers, all shared their memories about him around the dinner table. I've been hearing those stories for so long now, it's impossible for me to distinguish between what I remember and what I've been told.''

Summer heard the thread of pain in his voice and found herself wondering what it would be like to have grown up without the love and protection of her father. Though her relationship with her mother and sister was prickly at times, she'd always been able to count on her father to be there for her.

''What a remarkable family, to have kept his memory alive so long. Your mother and father must have shared a deep, abiding love.''

Cam nodded. ''You can see it in her eyes, even now, when she talks about him. It's as though the years fall away and he's still here with her.''

''She's a lucky woman.''

Cam fell silent. Then he pushed away from the table and began stacking the dishes.

Summer touched a hand to his. ''I'll clear the table later.''

''Sorry. I can't sit back and ignore the clutter. It's just not the Lassiter way. We'll do this together.'' He eyed the half-empty bottle of champagne. ''Then we'll watch the sun set while I ply you with chocolate and alcohol.''

She laughed. "Sounds serious."

"You bet." He brushed a kiss over her cheek before heading toward the balcony door.

As he disappeared inside, Summer went very still, wondering at the little tremors that raced along her spine. Anticipation hummed through her.

She picked up the rest of the dishes and tried to act casual as she deposited them on the counter. Beside her, Cam was loading the dishwasher. She studied the muscles that bunched and flexed across his back and shoulders as he worked.

She'd never before thought of kitchen work as erotic. But right now, this moment, she had the strangest urge to wrap her arms around his waist and press her lips to his throat.

Stunned at the image, she found herself laughing.

Cam looked up. "What?"

"Nothing." She swallowed her smile and turned away, busying herself with the coffeemaker.

When she did, Cam caught sight of that cool, pale expanse of flesh and wondered what Summer would do if he pressed a kiss just there.

The thought had him grinning.

She turned and arched a brow. "What?"

"Just thinking about dessert."

"You mean chocolate?"

"Something like that." He finished loading the dishwasher and took a step toward her.

Her eyes widened before she stepped back, feeling the edge of the counter against her flesh. "I'll have the coffee ready in a few minutes. In the meantime, if you'd like to pour the rest of the champagne, we can have it in the other room, or out on the balcony."

He could see her nerves and decided to play it her way. "Okay. Out on the balcony."

As he turned and walked away, she drew in a long, deep breath and wondered how she'd get through the rest of the evening.

Chapter 8

"Here's the coffee." Summer stepped onto the balcony holding a sleek black tray. On it were a carafe, cream and sugar and two mugs.

Though Cam remained at the railing, his face in shadow, she could feel him watching her. It sent a tingle of excitement through her veins.

She glanced at the two flutes. "Would you prefer champagne or coffee?"

He shrugged. "Whatever you're having."

"Coffee then." It was safer. Just having him close had her head spinning. The last thing she needed was anything that would further muddle her brain.

She filled the mugs. "Cream or sugar?"

"Black."

She carried the two mugs to the railing and handed one to him, feeling again the quick little slice of heat along her arm when their fingers brushed.

He drank. "I like what you've done here, Summer."

"Thanks." She smiled in the gathering darkness. "I figure sooner or later I'll have to give in and buy a house. One with a yard big enough for all the flowers I'm dying to plant."

"Why didn't you stay at your parents' house in Georgetown?"

"Because it isn't mine. I want something of my own." She looked over. "I spent better than half my childhood in boarding schools, here and in Europe, while my parents established themselves in the art community and stocked their galleries. When I finally earned my degree I vowed that I'd find a place where I could put down roots."

"Have you found it?"

She shrugged. "Not yet. But I'll know when I see it."

Cam nodded. "That's what happened to me.

I love the rolling hills and green countryside around this part of the country. That's why I chose Virginia. It's hard to beat the view. Of course—'' he set down his mug and turned to her ''—the view from here's not bad, either.''

She could feel the heat rush to her cheeks and was grateful for the growing darkness. ''You like teasing me, don't you?''

''Who said I'm teasing?''

''You just want to see how I'll react when you say something unexpected.''

''Unexpected?'' He smiled in the darkness, showing gleaming teeth. ''Summer, you have to know by now that I'm attracted, or I wouldn't be here.''

''Well, of course, but...''

''Does it go both ways?''

She nearly spilled her coffee. ''You're doing it again.''

''Doing what?''

''Throwing me off balance.''

''Good.'' He stepped closer, slipping his hands around her waist. ''Admit it. You're attracted to me.''

''Well, why wouldn't I be?'' Afraid the cup might slip from her hands, she set it on the balcony railing. "You're so smooth and slick and sure of yourself."

"Not to mention how handsome and charming I am."

When she chuckled he brushed his mouth over hers, tasting, sampling.

She drew back. "You forgot self-assured and arrogant."

He merely smiled and drew her closer, teasing her lips with his. He seemed in no hurry as he took the kiss deeper, until he heard her little moan of pleasure.

His hands moved from her waist to her back.

At the touch of his fingers on her bare flesh, she could feel her heart take a sudden dip, then shift into overdrive.

There was such incredible heat wherever he touched her.

She'd wanted this. Wanted his mouth on hers. His hands on her. She'd known, when she'd asked him here, that this was where it might lead. But she'd never dreamed he would affect her like this. She couldn't recall the last time a simple kiss had left her so defenseless.

He had to know how he affected women. And

yet, he made her feel as if she were the only one.

His mouth moved over hers, his taste dark and so potently male she felt the jolt clear to her soul. Just beneath the smooth, polished surface, she could taste the danger. The excitement. It had the breath backing up in her lungs and her heart thundering in her temples.

In some small corner of her mind she felt a warning that she was losing all control. This wasn't like her. She was a woman who was always in complete control. And yet, instead of her usual need to pull back, she found herself sliding deeper into the temptation he offered.

He changed the angle of his kiss. She was incredibly arousing to watch. The way she tried to plant her feet and, instead, leaned into him. The way her voice turned haughty before lowering to a purr of pleasure. The way her lashes fluttered, then closed as he deepened the kiss. The way her breath hitched in her throat, then ended on a sigh.

He turned slightly, leaning against the railing as his hands skimmed her back, then moved up her sides until his thumbs found her breasts.

When she started to pull away his mouth cov-

ered hers. Her breath mingled with his, and he
drew in the taste of her. Champagne and chocolate. Tart and sweet. A man could get drunk on
just her taste.

He could feel the blood roaring in his temples
as he brought his lips to her ear. She responded
with a sigh, and her hands tightened at his waist,
as if needing to anchor herself.

"I want you, Summer."

"I know. And I want..." She froze at the
ringing of her phone.

"Don't answer it." Cam bit lightly at her
lobe. Tugged. "Stay here with me and let me
show you all the things..."

The phone rang again, and Summer pushed
free of his arms. "I have to answer it, Cam."
Her voice sounded breathy in her own ears.

She turned away, walking across the balcony
like someone in a dream.

Cam stayed where he was, his breath coming
hard and fast as he heard her say, "Hello. Oh,
Dad. I do?" She gave a short laugh. "Yes. I
guess I am. I was...running to catch the phone."

Cam watched as she turned on a lamp, flood-
ing the room with light. She stood in a pool of

liquid gold, twirling the phone cord around and around her finger.

"I see." She took in a long, deep breath, trying to quiet the unsteady drumming of her heart. "I'm sorry. I was looking forward to dinner tomorrow night. How long will you be gone?"

She looked into the darkness, trying to see Cam on the balcony. He was swallowed up by the night. "Then I'll see you when you get back. I'll miss you. Have a safe flight."

She turned slightly, so that Cam could see her profile. "I love you, too, Dad."

She replaced the receiver, then stood a moment before walking to the door.

Her voice was stronger. "My father has to leave in the morning for Dublin."

"I'm sorry. I know you were looking forward to seeing him before he left."

She nodded. "Well, at least his phone call was timely."

"What's that supposed to mean?"

She smiled. "It bought me enough time to come to my senses."

"Yeah." There was no answering smile as he crossed the balcony, pausing at the open doorway to touch a finger to her cheek. "You strike me as the sensible type."

She thought of the boyhood he'd described. The tough, angry kid who resorted to fighting to hide his pain. There was some of that boy now in his eyes. The heat. The passion. It frightened her even while it attracted her.

"I can't be rushed, Cam. I need time to think through what I'm doing. What we're doing."

"We're doing what comes naturally to a man and woman."

"To you, maybe." She looked at her hands and realized they were trembling. "I don't want to do something I'll regret later."

He didn't know why that should grab him by the heart and tug. But it did. And that worried him. He'd always enjoyed women. All women. And when the attraction ended, as it inevitably had to, he'd always been able to move on with no regrets.

The thought of that happening with Summer was like a fist in the stomach.

To cover his confusion he brushed past her and picked up the box of chocolates. "Yeah. I'd hate for you to have any regrets. You take all the time you need, Summer." He held out the box. "Help yourself. I'm told they're the next best thing to sex."

She chose a chocolate-covered cherry and took a bite, all the while studying his eyes. They looked dark, dangerous. Challenging. "Not a bad substitute."

His smile was quick and equally dangerous. "If you believe that, something's been missing from your life."

"And you'd love to be the one to show me."

He gave a slight nod of his head. "You've got that right."

Forcing herself to relax, Summer selected another chocolate. "I think I'll stick with something safe."

"Safe is boring. Sometimes you just have to jump off a cliff and see whether or not you can fly."

"This doesn't sound like Stern Hayes Wheatley's hotshot young lawyer talking."

"Maybe that guy isn't real." He set the box of candy aside and took her hand in his.

She thought about pulling free, but it was too late. He'd already felt the quick jerk of her pulse. Just touching him, her hand was vibrating.

"You're shaking, Summer."

"You're playing with my nerves."

"It isn't your nerves I want."

"No. It's my body."

"Such a perfect body." He slid a thumb over her unsteady pulse. "But I've decided I want more."

"I don't…"

"It's your heart I want, Summer." He looked up and saw that her eyes were wide with surprise. But she was no more surprised than he was. Where had such thoughts come from? He couldn't recall ever saying such a thing before. He'd never before wanted more than a quick tumble, a little fun, before moving on to the next challenge.

Hearts weren't supposed to be part of the game. His or hers.

Her head came up in that way he'd come to recognize. Her tone turned frosty. "You know all the right words, don't you, Cam?"

"I try."

"Well, try this." She stepped back, breaking contact. Her pulse rate was so unsteady, she wondered if it would ever return to normal. "I've never been careless with my heart or my love. I'm not about to start now. So don't push.

I need time. A lot of time. And if you're a gentleman, you'll give me the time I need.''

"You want a gentleman?" He stepped closer and brushed a quick kiss on her cheek. Then, before she could react, he lifted her hand to his mouth and brushed another kiss across her knuckles, then turned her hand palm up, where he placed a kiss inside and closed her fingers to seal it inside.

"Don't be fooled by the clothes, Summer. Beneath the designer suit beats the heart of a rebel. I'm afraid that's about all the gentlemanly behavior I can manage tonight." He walked to the door. "Thanks for dinner. It was great."

As he started down the hall Summer yanked open the door to call, "Will I see you tomorrow?"

He turned. There was a strange light in his eyes, though she wasn't certain if was anger or amusement. "That depends."

"On what?"

"On who you want to see. Your version of a perfect gentlemen? Or the real Cameron Lassiter? The choice is yours."

Summer listened as his footsteps faded. She

closed the door and leaned against it, letting that scene on the balcony play through her mind.

She had no doubt where it would have ended if they hadn't been interrupted by the telephone.

She honestly couldn't tell if she was relieved or sorry. But she knew one thing. If Cam ever kissed her like that again, she wouldn't have the will to resist. In truth, she wanted the same thing he did.

At the moment she was feeling more confused than ever. And miserably unhappy.

Chapter 9

Cam rolled off the sofa and made his way to the kitchen, where he plugged in the coffee-maker. The decorator had arranged the appliances tastefully, to blend with the gleaming kitchen counters. Not a speck of dust marred the marble floor.

He took no notice of his spotless surroundings.

He'd wanted to be alone last night. And so he'd come to his new house. Aware that the bedroom set still hadn't been delivered, he'd settled down on the plush sofa. Instead of sleeping, he'd passed the time reading Alfonso Johnson's court transcripts. He'd wanted, more than anything, to find them clean. He wanted the man to be, in his own mind, guilty without a doubt, so that he could get back to work at Stern Hayes Wheatley without any more distractions.

Instead he'd found vague questions forming in his mind while reading through the pages and pages of testimony. A police informant had fingered Alfonso Johnson as the triggerman in the robbery gone wrong. The informant, up on drug charges, had his sentence reduced after cooperating with the investigators.

Cam knew how that worked. Over the years he'd found that more than half the informants would say whatever they were coached to say in order to get favorable treatment from the courts.

Then there were Alfonso's wife and mother, openly hostile to one another, each refuting the other's testimony until the authorities had been unable to believe either one of them.

When the coffee was ready Cam filled a mug and leaned a hip against the counter, deep in thought. It looked like he was about to do the one thing he'd been trying to avoid at all costs.

He picked up his cell phone and dialed his mother's number.

"Hello."

How could anyone sound that cheerful so early in the morning?

"Mom." He could hear the clatter of pots and pans in the background and despite his grim mood found himself smiling.

"Cameron. Did the bedroom furniture finally arrive?"

"No. But the sofa's not bad."

"You know you can always sleep here."

"I know. But I wanted some quiet time to read Alfonso's court transcripts."

"I see."

He heard the silent question and cleared his throat. "I've found enough questions to want to look into his case further."

"Oh, Cameron." He could hear the relief in his mother's voice. And something more. Understanding. "I know how hard this is for you."

"Yeah, well, I figure if you can deal with it, so can I."

Her tone softened. "Your grandfather wonders if you'll join us for breakfast."

Cam chuckled. "Not a chance. I'm far enough

away this morning that he can't bully me. But I'll see you both for dinner some time this week.''

"I'll tell him." She paused. "Has Tio's social worker made a decision yet on whether or not he can stay with his grandmother?''

"Not yet." He grinned. "But I'm working on that, too. I'll talk to you soon.''

He hung up the phone and stood a moment, debating whether or not to phone Summer. He wanted to hear her voice. Hell, who was he kidding? He wanted her here with him. In his arms. In his bed.

Annoyed, he walked to the shower. He had a full day ahead of him. The last thing he needed was the vision of Summer playing through his mind when he had to focus on work.

"Kathy."

At the sound of Cam's voice his assistant paused in the doorway.

He gave an apologetic grin. "I know I've been pushing this morning, but I'm about to ask for more. Would you send a messenger over to the court to get the rest of Alfonso Johnson's transcripts? I want everything, from his very first trial at the age of sixteen to the one that sent him away for life.''

She nodded.

''And I'd like you to phone the prison and request a lawyer-client meeting this afternoon.''

When she was gone he shoved from his desk and walked to the window where he stared at the pretty paths lined with flowers and flowing with pedestrians without really seeing them. He knew that the prestige of his firm would get him the meeting he requested, even though such things were routinely denied, especially on such short notice. He had no qualms about using that influence when he deemed it necessary.

Minutes later, when his assistant returned to say that the meeting had been arranged for three o'clock, he acknowledged without turning around.

He hadn't wanted to meet Alfonso Johnson. Now he would not only meet him, but be forced to look into the eyes of a man who'd been convicted of killing a police officer. An officer who had, like his own father, given up his life in the line of duty.

The only reason he was willing to do so was

that he had become convinced there was at least a slim chance the man doing time wasn't guilty.

Now to prove it to his own satisfaction. One way or the other.

The sun had long ago set when Cam climbed into his car and started the long drive home. The only good thing about it was that rush-hour traffic had dissolved to a trickle. He had the highway practically to himself.

He rolled his shirtsleeves and lowered the windows, allowing the evening breeze to fill his lungs. The thing that always bothered him the most about these prison visits was the fetid air. As though it had been sucked up by desperate men, then exhaled over and over, until every breath of stale air he breathed carried the taste of prison.

As he headed closer to the city he picked up his cell phone and dialed.

"Hello." The sound of Summer's voice had him visibly relaxing.

"Tell me you're sitting on your balcony, sipping champagne and nibbling chocolates."

"Close." She laughed, a clear sound that went straight to his heart. "It's iced tea. And I allowed myself only one chocolate."

"I'm not surprised. You always play by the rules, don't you?"

Hearing the weariness in his tone, her voice softened. "Where are you, Cam?"

"On my way home from prison."

"You drove Tio to see his father today?"

"Tio wasn't with me. I went alone."

"I see." Suddenly alert, she set aside her glass. "Want to tell me why?"

"To please my mother, I finally read the transcript from Alfonso Johnson's trial. Then I had my first face-to-face visit with him."

"That must mean that you think he's innocent."

"Not at all. It just means I'm not entirely convinced he had a fair trial. There's a difference, Summer."

"What did you think of him?"

Cam thought about the jolt he'd experienced at their meeting. He'd prepared himself to encounter anger, bitterness, depression. He'd found all that and more. Alfonso Johnson was a simmering cauldron of hatred at the judicial system he felt had betrayed him. He'd seemed genuinely surprised when Cam suggested that he was looking for legitimate reasons for requesting a new trial, but had offered little in his own defense.

As the silence dragged on Summer said softly, "You're tired. Why don't you come over and I'll fix a late supper."

Cam ran a hand through his hair. "Sorry. Not tonight. I'm hot and sweaty and I smell like prison."

"I don't care about that, Cam. I want to hear everything."

He felt an unexpected jolt of pleasure. The truth was, he wanted to share his day with her.

"I'll stop by my place and shower and change. I can be there in an hour."

"As good as your word. One hour exactly. I like that in a man." Summer was standing in the doorway of her apartment, looking cool and re-gal in a long gauzy skirt and midriff top the color of a fresh peach.

Though she would never admit it, she'd been watching for him for the past twenty minutes.

"I didn't want to give you time to change your mind." He started past her, then stopped and breathed her in. "You smell good. Like roses."

Her heart did a hard, quick dip. "And you don't smell at all like prison."

"I showered. Otherwise you'd throw me out."

"Not a chance." She was laughing as she led him toward the kitchen. "I need you to open this bottle of Chardonnay."

"Oh, I see. You'll keep me around only as long as I can be useful."

"That's right." She handed him a corkscrew while she removed two stem glasses from a cupboard.

"Is there a reason for this wine?"

She held the glasses while he removed the cork and began pouring. "From the tone of your voice, I thought you might like to relax for a while on the balcony before you eat."

"Yeah." He touched his glass to hers. "I'd like that. What I'd like even better is to just sit and look at you."

As she led him out the door, Summer decided it was what she wanted, too.

"Now that you've had time to reflect, what do you think about Alfonso Johnson?" Summer sat back, sipping hot coffee. Over a leisurely meal on the balcony, she had carefully avoided any mention of Cam's visit to the prison until she thought he was ready to open up.

With each passing minute she had watched his energy return, and with it, his good humor.

Cam went silent, remembering. "I saw the suspicion in his eyes when I told him I was searching for enough compelling evidence to obtain a new trial. As you can imagine, seven years in prison can help a man store up a lot of anger and doubt. He's not ready to trust me." Cam ran a hand over his eyes. "But that's all right, because I'm not ready to trust him, either. We both have a long way to go. I told Alfonso that I needed him to begin writing down everything he could recall about that night. Names. Dates. Even the most insignificant details."

Summer rested her chin on her hands. "And he agreed?"

"Not exactly. He said he'd think about it. I told him not to think about it too long. Justice is notoriously slow, especially in granting another trial to a man convicted by a jury of his peers. To make him more amenable I promised him that if Tio doesn't miss any classes this week I'll drive him up for a visit."

"How did he respond to that?"

"He didn't say anything." Cam's hands tightened on the stem of his wineglass as he thought about the flare of heat in the man's eyes. It had been brief. No more than a second. But in that instant there had been such an air of hope mingled with the doubt.

How would a man, imprisoned for years on a charge that might have been false, react if the courts refused to hear his petition? To save his sanity, a man in that situation wouldn't allow himself to be tempted with the idea. It was self-preservation to reject it. But in the dark recesses of his heart, even a hardened prisoner like Alfonso Johnson would nurse a flicker of hope. But if Cam should fail, the anger, the resentment, would fester and become even more inflamed.

He wouldn't let himself think about that now. He'd taken that first step. But he knew, from experience with cases like this, that there would be miles ahead of him.

At the mysterious smile on her lips he arched a brow. "Secrets?"

She shrugged. "Maybe you should ask me about my day."

"Sorry." He reached across the table and

took her hand in his. "I've been boring you with all this."

"I wasn't bored, Cam. I wanted to hear everything."

"And it felt good to share. Now tell me everything about your day."

Her smile grew. The touch of his hand on hers was exactly what she'd been craving. "I had planned on turning in my report on Tio today. I've decided to recommend, at least for now, that he be allowed to remain with his grandmother."

"That's great, Summer." He closed her hand between both of his and stared into her eyes. "I hope you aren't doing this just for me."

She shook her head. "I'm doing it because it's the right thing to do. Tio deserves a chance to know his father. And now that you think Alfonso may get a new trial, it's even more important that father and son remain in close contact." Her smile faded slightly. "But I'm afraid there's a new twist in Tio's case. There was a letter in the morning's mail. A letter with no return address, though it bore a Washington, D.C., postmark. The writer claimed to be Tio Johnson's mother, Jobina, seeking custody of her son."

Cam gave a long, deep sigh. One more complication in an already complicated case. "Why would this woman come forward now?"

"I was wondering the same thing. Do you think she's been keeping track of Tio and his father all these years?"

He shrugged. "Could be. Or maybe she has someone on the inside at the prison. A guard or a staff member who lets her know when there's any interest in Alfonso's case."

"Or maybe she's just got her life pulled together and wants to be a mother to her son again."

Cam shrugged. "Maybe." He pushed away from the table. "Come on. I'll help you clean up."

Before he could start stacking the plates she put a hand on his arm. "We can do that later."

"Later?" He glanced over.

The strange Mona Lisa smile on her face had him going perfectly still.

She moved close until her body barely skimmed his and lifted her face. Her voice was a low purr. "Kiss me, Cam. Quick. Before I lose my nerve."

Once, when he'd been about eight, he'd come

barreling out of his upstairs bedroom eager to join in a neighborhood sandlot baseball game. At the top of the stairs he'd encountered Micah's skateboard and had flipped end over end all the way down. As he lay, dazed and battered at the bottom of the stairs, he'd felt as if all the air had been squeezed from his lungs.

He felt the same way now.

It was on the tip of his tongue to refuse. Except that she was already wrapping her arms around his neck and brushing her mouth on his. He kissed her, feeling all the blood in his body rush to his loins.

Through a mist of heat and desire he brought his hands up to hers and peeled her away. "Wait a minute. Wait just a minute."

"Cam, I..." She leaned in, but he held her just short of her goal.

"You said last night you wanted a gentleman."

"I know I said that, but..."

He shook his head. "Sorry. You've got the wrong guy. Especially tonight. When a man spends a day in prison, some of that's bound to rub off."

As he released her hands and took a step back,

she smiled. Her voice took on that haughty tone he'd come to recognize. "You're not getting rid of me that easily, Lassiter."

"Really?" His eyes narrowed. "What're you going to do? Bar the door so you can have your way with me?"

"If I have to." Laughing, she crossed the room and stood in front of the door. "I invited you here tonight because I've had time to think it over. I want you, Cam. And you want me."

"Seems to me that was my line."

"Yeah." Her smile grew. "I decided if it was good enough for you, it's good enough for me."

He walked to her until they were mere inches apart. "Don't kid yourself. I wasn't joking. I can't be the gentleman you hoped for. And if you let me love you, you'll have to accept me the way I am, rough edges and all."

She touched a hand to his cheek. Just a touch, but she felt him jerk back as though burned. That only made her bolder. Reaching out, she brushed her fingers over his mouth until his eyes narrowed on her with a fire that had her heart racing.

His voice was little more than a whisper. "I hope you know what you're doing."

"I do."

Before she knew what was happening his arms were around her, dragging her so close she could feel his heartbeat inside her own chest.

"Then hold on, Summer. It's going to be one hell of a night."

Chapter 10

He drew her close and took her mouth with his. There was an urgency to the kiss that was unlike all the others. He'd always held something back before, afraid to let her see the depth of his passion. Now he was free to touch, to taste, to take. And he did. With a thoroughness that had her gasping.

She drew back slightly, her eyes wide.

His smile sent her heart tumbling. "Afraid?"

"No, I..." She swallowed, then, feeling steadier, shook her head. "No."

"That's good." There was a glint of something dangerous in his eyes. "Because it's too late."

"Are you saying that to frighten me, Cam?"

"Consider it a warning." He dragged her into his arms.

The hands at her shoulders were almost bruising as he gathered her close and plundered her mouth. She felt the quick jolt of nerves, then the rush of heat and energy as her blood surged through her veins. She sighed as he changed the angle of the kiss and took it deeper. Took her higher. Then higher still.

This was what she'd wanted. What she'd thought about whenever she thought of Cam. The flash. The fire. The rough, churning need sparking through her. He'd been right to warn her. There was nothing soft or easy about the feelings he'd unleashed. But she welcomed them, as she welcomed the feel of his mouth on hers. His hands moving over her added to the excitement as they touched and teased and tempted. And tormented.

She offered her lips with a hunger she never knew she possessed. "Touch me, Cam. Take me." The words tumbled from between her lips, surprising her as much as him.

"You mean hard and fast and quick?" He gave a mirthless laugh. "That's too easy." He lifted a finger to stroke her cheek. "Do you know how many nights I've lost sleep over you?"

She tried to laugh, but her throat felt constricted. "Probably no more than I did."

"It's nice to know I wasn't alone in my fantasies. But I doubt yours were anywhere near as exciting as mine." He framed her face and stared deeply into her eyes. "You have no idea the things I've wanted to do with you. To you."

His eyes were so hot and fierce, she felt a quick lightning flash of fear skitter along her spine.

Her voice was little more than a whisper. "Show me."

He seemed to consider a moment before his hands came around her, cupping her hips as he dragged her roughly against him. With his mouth on hers he took her on a wild, reckless ride. She could feel herself climbing, climbing, so high it left her gasping. Just as suddenly she was falling.

She wrapped her arms around his waist and held on for the ride of her life. She gasped when she realized she'd been backed against the door. And still his mouth moved over hers, while his hands, those strong, clever hands, moved over her at will, stroking, arousing until she was half-mad with desire.

"Cam. Please." She could barely get the words out. Her breathing was labored, her heart pounding furiously in her chest.

"Not yet. I've waited so long. So long." He brought his mouth to her throat and ran wet, nibbling kisses along the sleek column of her neck.

She sighed, and tipped her head back, giving him easier access. The sound that escaped her lips reminded him of a lazy cat dozing in the sun. But there was nothing lazy about the way her body moved against his.

He pressed soft, feathery kisses over her collarbone, then lower, until his lips closed around one erect nipple. Despite the barrier of the soft cotton midriff, he nibbled and suckled until she felt her knees buckle.

She clutched at his waist to keep herself anchored.

He reached a hand to the buttons of her shirt, all the while watching her eyes. When he slid the fabric from her shoulders, he encountered silk and lace. In one smooth motion he tugged it aside to reveal pale, smooth skin that had his throat going dry. He unfastened the long skirt and watched as it drifted to the floor to pool at her feet. Now there was only a tiny strip of lace, which soon joined the rest of her clothes.

Moonlight filtered through the balcony windows, gilding her flesh, bathing her in a golden glow.

"You're so beautiful, Summer. I've waited so long to see all that cool, white skin." His eyes glinted with a dangerous light. "To touch it." He ran his hands over her and felt her tremble. "To taste it." He brought his mouth to her breast.

The nipple hardened instantly at his touch.

Without warning he found her, hot and wet, and brought her to the first peak.

Stunned and reeling, all she could do was clutch blindly at him and hold on while he took her to places she'd never been before. She would surely have fallen except for his hands, and the cold, smooth wood of the door behind her. With lips and teeth and tongue he moved over her, making her aware of feelings she'd never known she possessed.

"Cam. Wait. I need to..." She tugged his shirt over his head, needing to touch him the way he was touching her.

Excitement rippled through her as she passed a hand over his hair-roughened chest. Felt the way his muscles bunched and tightened as she gripped his arms. His stomach quivered when she reached for the snaps at his waistband. It thrilled her to know that he was so affected by her touch.

When his clothes had joined hers on the floor, he drew her close until she could feel the imprint of his body on hers. They came together in a kiss so hot, so hungry, she wondered that they didn't devour each other.

He framed her face with his hands. The look in his eyes had her heart leaping to her throat.

"I've tried to be gentle, Summer. But I can't hold back any longer."

If this was holding back, she wondered what it would be like when he let himself go. Her words tumbled out between strained breaths. "I don't need you to be easy, Cam. I just need you."

He lifted her, intending to take her to the bedroom. But the need was too great. Instead he paused to kiss her again and found himself dropping to his knees, dragging her down with him. His kisses were no longer gentle, his hands no longer careful as they moved over her with an intensity that had her gasping.

They came together in a firestorm of passion and need. Breathing shallow. Heartbeats thundering. Bodies slick.

The world beyond this room no longer mattered. The night air filtering through the screen was sweet with the masses of flowers on the balcony. The water from the fountain was a soothing backdrop. Crickets chirped, and a moth beat its wings against the screen. But the man and woman locked in each other's embrace took no notice.

Summer sighed. No man had ever made her feel like this. With a kiss he could erase all the cares of the day. With a single touch he could make her shudder.

One minute she felt calm, cool, settled. The next she felt her heartbeat beginning to speed up, her breath burning her throat as she struggled to hold back the desperate need that had taken hold of her senses.

Cam forced himself to move slowly. To taste.

To savor. He brought his mouth to her breast, to nibble and suckle, until she writhed and moaned and clutched at his head. Then he moved to the other breast, to tease, to torment. He thought of all the fantasies that had crowded his mind since he met her. None could even come close to this flesh-and-blood woman in his arms.

She lay, steeped in pleasure, her eyes heavy-lidded with passion. By the light of the stars that filtered into the room she was like a fairy-tale princess, a goddess whose hair was touched with gold, whose skin was pale as milk. Her eyes were large and luminous, touched with moon glow. And fixed on him with rapt attention.

It thrilled him to know that it was his touch she craved. His name she whispered. His. Only his. That knowledge fueled his passion and touched his heart in a way he'd never believed possible.

The thought of taking her now, and ending this terrible torment, was almost more than he could resist. But he'd waited so long. Wanted so desperately.

His hands moved over her, watching the way the storm inside her was reflected in her eyes. It was exciting to watch as it gathered strength, gathered fury. He bent his mouth to her breast. Teased. And watched as she let herself ride the storm.

Her lips parted, and she tried to speak his name, though no words came out. Still he held back, wanting to drive her, and himself, to the very edge of madness. And he did. With lips and tongue and fingertips he took her up, then over. And then, giving her no time to recover, took her again.

She was wonderful to watch. Her eyes glazed over, and she reached blindly for him. This time he let her draw him to her. Found her mouth with his. Laced his fingers with hers as he entered her.

And then he was drowning in her. Caught in a whirlpool of his own making. He breathed in the fresh, clean fragrance of summer flowers. Filled his lungs with her even while he filled her body.

The depth of her arousal caught her by surprise. She wrapped herself around him, feeling each long, deep thrust all the way to her core. Then she was moving with him, climbing with him.

"Summer." Her name was torn from his lips.

At the sound of that hoarse cry, she struggled through a haze of passion to focus on him. All she could see were midnight-blue eyes, fixed on her with such intensity. All she could hear was the way his heartbeat matched hers. Thundering wildly out of control.

They moved together. Climbed together. They felt such incredible strength as, with breathing labored, hearts racing, they took that final step into space.

And soared.

"That was—" Cam took in a long, deep breath "—amazing." He buried his lips in the little hollow between her neck and shoulder. "And so are you."

Summer lay perfectly still, waiting to settle. In her whole life she'd never had an experience to compare with this. Had the floor shifted? Had the building tilted? She felt wildly disoriented. Completely out of focus.

She felt like standing on her balcony and shouting to the world. She felt like weeping. She felt too drained to move.

As the silence dragged on Cam looked at her with concern. "Am I too heavy?"

"No." She lifted a hand to his hair, loving the feel of it against her fingertips.

"You're awfully quiet. I hope this doesn't mean you're sorry."

"Oh, Cam." She touched his cheek. "How could I be sorry after something so...wonderful."

He felt his heart begin to beat again and realized he'd been holding his breath, afraid that, in his passion, he'd hurt her.

"Sorry about the floor." He glanced over. "I guess I could have made it as far as the sofa. I wasn't thinking very clearly."

Summer gave a laugh, as clear as a bell. "There wasn't a thing wrong with your thinking. It was as muddled as mine. Maybe next time we'll try the sofa."

He cocked a brow. "Next time?"

"I was hoping..." She started to push away until his hand on her arm stilled her movements. She knew she was blushing. "I thought you might like to stay the night."

"You've got that right." He was grinning like a fool. "Wild horses couldn't drag me away now." He rolled aside, then drew her into the circle of his arms. "If you'll give me a minute to catch my breath, we'll try out the sofa. Or the bed. Your choice.''

She was laughing, as much from relief as from his typical male attitude. ''Are you suggesting that in just a minute you'll be able to work all that...magic again?''

''You're having some doubts, Ms. O'Connor?''

''You didn't tell me you were a superhero.''

''I didn't think I had to. I thought you knew.''

''Uh-huh.'' Still laughing, she leaned up on one elbow, her fingers playing with the mat of hair on his chest. ''What I know is that you're very sure of yourself.''

''At least where you're concerned. There's never been a doubt.'' He folded his hands behind his head and gave a contented smile. ''Do you know what I thought, that first time I saw you in my mother's office?''

Intrigued, she leaned closer. ''What did you think?''

''That I'd just run into Joan of Arc, burning with zeal and ready to go to war.''

She nodded. ''Close. Maybe not about being Joan of Arc. But I was certainly ready to do battle with the hotshot lawyer who thought he was so smart.''

His smile grew. "I could tell. You practically had flames shooting out of those beautiful eyes. You were such a contradiction. All prim and buttoned up. And then I saw those fabulous legs and I knew I was hooked.''

She glanced down. "It was my legs?" She turned to him and fluttered her lashes. "And here I thought it was my great mind that turned you on.''

"That, too." He brushed a hand down her hair, then drew her close for a long, lingering kiss that had them both sighing.

When they came up for air, he scrambled to his feet and lifted her into his arms.

She snuggled close and turned her face to his throat. "Where are we going?''

He gasped for breath, loving the feel of her lips on his flesh. "I was hoping to make it to your bed. But when you do that thing with your mouth against my throat, I lose control.''

"You mean this?" She brushed soft kisses across his neck and shoulder, causing him to moan.

"I think we'd better settle for the sofa.''

"It's pretty narrow."

"That's all right. For what I have in mind, we won't need much space. Besides, I'll never make it to the bedroom."

"Why, Mr. Lassiter." She wrapped her arms around his neck and nipped at his shoulder. "You really *are* a superhero, aren't you?"

His grin was absolutely wicked. "I'll accept your apology for that sarcastic tone later. For now…" He lay her on the sofa and stretched out beside her.

"For now?"

"This. Just this." His mouth crushed hers.

There was no need for words as they took each other once more into that dark, delicious world that lovers have known from the beginning of time.

Chapter 11

"Where are you going?" Feeling the mattress shift, Cam reached out and snagged Summer's wrist before she could slip away. In the darkness he could read the bedside clock. It was almost three in the morning.

"I'm hungry. I thought I'd hunt up some food."

"And here I thought your only hunger was for me."

She laughed and leaned over him, brushing a kiss to his mouth. "I have to admit. You've made me aware of an appetite I never knew I had."

"Now that's what a guy likes to hear." He pulled her into his arms and ran soft, teasing kisses up her cheek to her ear, loving the way she shivered and snuggled closer into his arms.

Sometime during the night they'd finally made it to her bed, where they'd alternately loved and dozed, then loved again. Each time they awoke, the need was there. As sharp, as demanding as any hunger.

At times it felt as though they'd been together for a lifetime, and the loving had been soft and easy. At other times their passion had exploded like a sudden, violent summer storm, with flashes of lightning and heart-stopping thunder that left them drained and spent.

She started to push from his arms. "I thought I'd make some coffee and toast a bagel."

"I'll help." Instead of releasing her, he nipped playfully at her lobe. "In just a minute."

His warm breath made her tremble. "Cam." She tried to pull away, and he tightened his arms around her before lowering his head to run soft, nibbling kisses across her throat.

Her voice thickened. "You know what this always leads to."

"Yeah." He trailed his mouth across her shoulder. "I'm counting on it."

She sighed, feeling her body respond. Already that warm, languid feeling had stolen quietly over her, robbing her of the will to resist. "You're not playing fair."

"You got that right." He combed his fingers through her hair, loving the way she looked in his arms.

Then he proceeded to show her, with slow, deep kisses and touches as soft and fine as a whisper, all the things that were in his heart.

Summer awoke to the wonderful rich aroma of coffee. She opened her eyes to see dawn light spreading ribbons of fire across the horizon. Though the morning air drifting in the open window was pleasantly cool, there was already a hint of the heat and humidity to come.

"Morning, sleepyhead." Cam set a cup of coffee on the night table and sat on the edge of the bed before leaning down to brush a kiss over her lips.

"Morning. Nice of you to let me sleep."

"Nice of you to let me—" he gave her a heart-stopping grin "—enjoy such a memorable night."

"It was memorable." She sat up and reached for the coffee. "Mmm. Now, that's good. Almost as good as your kisses. I may let you make my coffee every morning."

"Promise?"

At the intense look in his eyes she felt herself flushing. She hadn't thought beyond the night. Nor did she want to. What they'd shared had been special. But one night of loving was no guarantee of anything more. Especially with a man of Cameron Lassiter's reputation.

To cover her confusion she glanced around. "No bagel?"

He shook his head. "I checked the refrigerator and freezer. No bagels. But I did find this." He held out a plate of cheese and crackers.

"Oh, that's perfect. Just what I need to restore my energy."

"Yeah. That's what I figured." He was smiling as he offered her a bite. "I'd be a fool not to see to that."

She narrowed her eyes. "Always thinking, aren't you, Lassiter?"

"That's right. One of us has to see to the really important details. Food. Drink. Sex."

She helped herself to another bite. "Just like

a guy. Always thinking with a certain part of his anatomy.''

''It's our duty. How else are we supposed to go forth and multiply?''

''If it were left up to women, I'm sure we'd find an easier way.''

He laughed. ''Easier, maybe. But not nearly as much fun.'' He took the cup from her hands and set it on the night table. ''Speaking of fun...''

She held out her hands to keep him at bay. ''Cam, we have to think about getting ready for work.''

''Work?'' He dragged her into his arms and brushed her lips with his. At once he felt the jolt. ''Woman, I can't be thinking about such mundane things when duty is calling.''

They were both laughing as they came together in a searing kiss. But their laughter suddenly dissolved into sighs, and then to moans.

Cam found himself wondering how he could possibly get through the day without touching her like this. Holding her. Loving her.

Love. He pushed aside the thought and lost himself in her.

Later, as he stood on the balcony sipping

strong, hot coffee, the thought returned to mock him. Hadn't he recently boasted to Pop that he much preferred the woman of the moment to the woman of a lifetime? When he'd said that, he'd surely meant it. Words like love, commitment, were for others. After all, he'd learned early on that it was possible to lose, in the blink of an eye, the most important person in his life.

A man didn't set himself up to take a beating a second time. Did he?

Something was happening here. Something he didn't want to probe too deeply.

"Breakfast is ready."

At the sound of Summer's voice he turned.

"I don't have bagels, but I do have almond cherry muffins. We can eat them out on the balcony."

She was wearing a simple navy skirt and white blouse, her hair scooped behind one ear with a jeweled comb. He found himself speechless at the sight of her. Quite simply, she took his breath away.

She set down the plate of muffins and walked to him, touching a hand to his cheek. "You all right?"

"I am now." He gathered her close and

brushed her mouth with his, then stepped back and drew in a breath, still tasting her. "Oh, yeah. I'm fine now."

She gave him a measured look as she took a seat at the small table. There had been something in his eyes. Something sad and wounded that had touched a chord in her.

She pointed to the thick manila folder by his elbow. "Is that Alfonso's file?"

He nodded. "The transcript from his trial."

"Have you found any discrepancy that might warrant a new trial?"

He shook his head. The frown line was back between his brows. "There are a lot of little things that don't add up. But nothing pivotal. I've gone over it too many times to count. I'm missing something. I don't know what. But I'm convinced if I keep reading, I'll eventually find it."

She reached for the file. "Mind if I scan it?"

He shrugged and reached for a muffin. "Help yourself."

He ate in silence, enjoying the way she looked as she absently reached for her coffee while poring over the pages of the transcript.

There was something pleasant and soothing

about spending the morning with a woman whose mind was as sharp as a razor even while she looked as fresh and as simple as one of her flowers. He glanced around and found himself smiling at the colorful blossoms spilling out of pottery bowls and vines trailing over the balcony railing. The air was sweet with the perfume of lilies, roses, honeysuckle. A bold finch watched him as it took a bath in the fountain's spray.

With just a few touches she'd been able to turn this cramped little apartment into a home, something he and a decorator had been unable to do with his fine big house. It occurred to him that it wasn't the space so much as the feeling that space conveyed. This place reflected Summer. The things she cared about. His new house was simply a reflection of a stranger's taste. There was nothing of him there. Probably because he hadn't wanted to reveal anything of himself. Hadn't it been that way with his life, so far? No strings. No commitments. Just passing through.

Absently he wandered inside and rinsed his coffee cup at the sink before heading to the shower. A short time later he stepped onto the balcony to retrieve his papers.

Summer's head came up. On her face was a look of contained excitement. "Did you notice that at the trial Alfonso's wife testified that she wasn't at home the night of the crime?"

Cam nodded. "That's right."

"But when the police arrested Alfonso, he told them he'd gone to the store for his wife. And when they went to his house, she answered the door."

Cam stepped closer to peer over Summer's shoulder. "There might have been enough time for her to return home between the exact hour of the crime and the time when the police arrived at Alfonso's house to check out his alibi."

"Maybe. But who's to say she ever left the house?" Summer pointed to the transcript. "If she did leave, as she claimed, that means she left her five-year-old son home alone."

Cam shrugged. "It happens. Not everyone is a caring, considerate parent. In your line of work I'm sure you hear about kids left home alone every day."

Summer nodded. "That's just it. In most cases the neglectful parent is willing to lie just to avoid the publicity, and sometimes the prosecution and penalty, that are certain to follow.

But here's a woman who could have provided an alibi for her husband, and along with it, proof that she was home with her son. Instead, she testified under oath that she'd left her little son home alone, and that paved the way for her husband to be found guilty of a brutal murder.''

Cam's eyes narrowed as he considered the implications. ''You think she set him up?''

Summer shook her head. ''I don't know what to think, Cam. But this is a woman who's now seeking custody of her son. If she truly loves him, why did she wait so long? And if she doesn't love him, why is she back to claim her parental rights now?''

He was nodding. ''Yeah. Why is she suddenly in the picture again?''

As she returned the pages to the folder and closed it, Cam lifted her hand to his mouth and kissed it. ''Thanks.''

''I haven't done anything.''

He linked her fingers with his, then looked into her eyes. ''You saw something I've been missing every time I read that transcript.''

''It could turn out to be nothing.''

''And it could turn out to be the key I've been

searching for. No matter what, it's nice to have someone who shares my interest in this case.''

She looked at their linked hands. ''I may still end up fighting to have Tio returned to his mother.''

''If you do, it'll be because you're convinced that it's best for him.''

''My, my.'' She touched a hand to his cheek. ''It wasn't that long ago you vowed to fight me with everything you had. How far you've come, Mr. Lassiter.''

He winked, sending her heart into a sudden spiral. ''How far we've both come, Ms. O'Connor.''

He picked up the file. ''Guess I'd better head home and get dressed for a day at the office.''

''I think you look just fine the way you are.''

He laughed. ''Thanks. But this doesn't quite fit the dress code. If I ever showed up at Stern Hayes Wheatley in jeans and a T-shirt they'd fire me on the spot.''

''It would be their loss.''

''My champion.'' He pulled her close and kissed her. He'd intended it to be a simple touch of mouth to mouth. But the minute their lips met, he felt the sudden rush of heat and couldn't seem to stop himself. Against her lips he whispered, "You've got me thinking I can take on the whole judicial system by myself. And win."

Summer could feel her head spinning. Could feel her blood slowly heating and her bones melting like hot wax. It was on the tip of her tongue to ask him to stay the day. She'd never missed a day of work. Would no more shirk her duty than steal. But in this man's arms she seemed to lose something of herself.

He lifted his head and took a step back. "Got to go. Will I see you tonight?"

She nodded, too overcome to speak.

"Okay." He brushed a hand down her hair, then picked up the file and crossed to the door.

"Wait." She dashed inside and fumbled in her purse until she found a key. When she held it out he merely looked at her.

She smiled. "In case you get off work before me. It might be nice to find you here waiting for me."

"Yeah. I'd like that, too." He looked thoughtful as he pocketed the key.

When he was gone she stood very still, taking several deep breaths to calm her ragged breathing.

She was in over her head. And what was worse, she didn't seem to mind in the least.

She danced around the apartment, locating her briefcase. She couldn't wait for the day to be over. She didn't care how much work she was handed. All that mattered was that tonight she and Cam would be together again. Laughing. Loving. And feeling gloriously, joyously alive.

Chapter 12

Cam pulled into traffic and pressed the auto dial on his car's speakerphone.

"Summer O'Connor here."

At the sound of her voice, the heat, the traffic and the work ahead of him seemed to fade away. "How's your day going?"

She sighed. "Pretty much as usual. I have six appointments and only time for four, which means I'll be going without lunch again. A woman claiming to be Tio's mother phoned, threatening to complain to my superiors if I don't act immediately on her request for custody of her son. When I explained that it all took time and that I'd need to do an in-home inspection, she hung up on me." Her tone carried a hint of weariness. "Just another day in the trenches. How's your day?"

"After last night, how could it be anything but perfect?" He ignored the blaring of a horn and grinned. "The powers that be at Stern Hayes Wheatley are so confident of the case I've prepared for the McGonnagle-Carlson trial, they think the other side will settle."

"Oh, Cam, that's wonderful."

"Maybe. I'd prefer to argue my case in front of a jury."

"Ever the fighter, aren't you?"

He laughed. "Yeah. In or out of the courtroom. But I'll leave the decision in the hands of others. Right now I'm heading up to another face-to-face with Alfonso Johnson. I want to see if I can jog his memory about his wife's testimony."

"What time do you think you'll be back?"

"I should be back in D.C. by early evening, in time to take you somewhere quiet and secluded for dinner."

"Hmm." Her schedule had just become much more tolerable. "Sounds good."

"Better than good. It'll be fantastic. And what I've planned for dessert won't be half-bad either, if a certain gorgeous creature is in the mood."

"I'm already in the mood. I'll see you tonight."

After she hung up, Cam adjusted his sunglasses and found himself smiling at the truck driver beside him. His day just kept getting better by the minute.

On the drive back to the city Cam punched the accelerator and cruised past the few cars that moved along the almost deserted highway. His suit jacket and tie lay discarded on the passenger seat. He'd rolled the sleeves of his shirt above the elbows and lowered the windows, breathing in the fresh air.

His meeting with Alfonso Johnson had been a disaster. The man's experiences with lawyers had left him unwilling to trust anyone who represented the law. He'd sat, tight-lipped, eyes burning into Cam's, without offering a word in his own defense. Even when Cam read Alfonso's own words proclaiming his innocence to the judge before sentencing, the prisoner refused to comment.

"So, Alfonso," Cam had prodded. "Are you innocent, like you claimed? Or are you doing the time you deserve?"

"You figure it out, smart man."

"According to testimony in your trial, the police found you standing over the body, gun in hand. Another man identified you as the gunman."

"Looks deceive, and men lie. And the law makes mistakes." Alfonso had pushed away from the table, signaling an end to their meeting.

Cam had enough experience with inmates to know that most of them proclaimed their innocence to anyone who would listen. Still, there were enough nagging doubts to make him want to delve deeper. To that end he'd already hired his brother's security firm to look into a few of the more troubling details. If anyone could dig up the truth, Cam thought, it was his brother Micah.

Now that his work was done, the rest of this day and night belonged to Summer.

Turning up the radio, he heard the voice of Percy Sledge, and joined him, singing at the top of his lungs about when a man loves a woman. A short time later he parked at the Northside Apartments and was out of the car in a flash, dashing toward the elevators.

He turned the key in the lock and stepped inside, surprised and pleased to see that Summer was already there, standing on the balcony. As he crossed the room he could still catch the faint whiff of her perfume lingering in the air. She hadn't changed. She was wearing the navy skirt and white blouse. The sight of her, all prim and buttoned up, had him smiling.

"I thought by now you'd have slipped into something comfortable."

She whirled to face him, hand at her throat. Her eyes went wide before she let out a long, slow breath. "I didn't hear you come in."

"Yeah. I can see that." He could see something else. The fear that had flashed in her eyes before she'd managed to control it. And the way her pulse was beating a frantic tattoo in her throat.

He ran a hand up her arm. "What's wrong, Summer?"

She let out a shaky breath. "There was a message on my machine when I got home."

When he merely arched a brow she led him into the kitchen and, without a word, flicked the switch, playing the tape.

"Little miss social worker." The voice was little more than a whisper. Low, menacing. "If you know what's good for you, you'll quit shuffling papers. Remember, I know where to find you."

Cam rewound it, playing it again. When it was finished he looked at Summer. "Has he ever called you before?"

She shook her head.

"Recognize the voice?"

"No."

"You think this is about Tio Johnson?"

She swallowed. Nodded. "I have plenty of other cases I'm working on. The caller was careful not to name names. But it sounds to me as though Alfonso Johnson has learned that his wife is seeking custody and he wants to make his feelings known about it." She could still see, in her mind's eye, the anger and bitterness that had emanated from him in bitter waves on her visit to prison. "He could have people on the outside watching out for his interests."

"Maybe." Cam rewound the tape, opened the

case, removed the tape and dropped it into his pocket. "The police will want this. Got a fresh tape?"

She fished in a kitchen drawer and held it up.

As he inserted it he said, "Pack whatever you'll need for the next couple of days."

"Pack? Cam, I'll call the police and report this. They'll look into it."

"That's right. They'll look into it. And maybe, in time, they'll even figure out who this character is. But in the meantime…" He took her hands. Despite the heat of the day, they were cold as ice. "You heard the man. He knows where you live. That's why he called you here at your apartment, rather than at your office or on your cell phone. He wanted you to know that he wasn't bluffing."

She nodded. "I'd figured out that much for myself."

"All right then." He led her toward the bedroom. "Let's go someplace where he can't find you."

"That would be?"

He gave her a quick, dangerous smile. "Didn't you mention you'd like to see my new house?"

* * *

She'd packed quickly, then accompanied Cam downstairs to his car. As he drove she sat watching his hands, firm and unshakable on the wheel. And his profile. Eyes steely. Teeth clamped. A little muscle working in his jaw.

Even if he hadn't told her about his past, she'd have known that he was a man who enjoyed a good fight. Though there had been little change in his expression, she'd sensed the thread of steel in his voice, in his manner, after he heard the threat.

He'd spoken to his brother Micah, who operated a security company. Following his directions, Cam had carefully walked around, looking for any sign of an intruder. From the little she'd overheard, Summer knew that an operative had already been assigned to watch her apartment. It gave her some comfort, but not much. She had a job to do. A life to live. And no anonymous voice on the phone was going to keep her from it.

They drove in silence through the rolling Virginia countryside. Whatever anger Cam felt seemed to disappear as he turned up a curving drive and parked in front of a graceful, sprawling house of buff brick. Arched windows stood in welcome on either side of double wooden doors.

"This is it?"

"Yeah."

"Oh, Cam." She stared around at the rolling lawn, seeing in her mind the perfect spot for a rose garden. And along the curve of walkway, lilies. "It's beautiful."

"Thanks." He tossed his sunglasses on the dash and rounded the hood of the car to open her door. "It lacks the warmth of your place, but it's pretty much put together. I haven't spent a lot of time here. I was told the new bed was just delivered some time this morning." He shot her a sideways glance as he caught her hand and led her up the low, stone steps. "This'll be my first time to try it out."

As he fitted the key in the lock he was surprised to see the door swing open.

Puzzled, he put a hand out to keep her from following. "Stay here."

He stepped inside before stopping in midstride.

The pictures had been torn from the walls and lay smashed around the room. The cushions of the new sofa had been slashed, the stuffing littering the floor. Shards of crystal were all that was left of an expensive imported lamp that had once stood on a round marble end table.

Cam swore as he picked his way through the debris toward the kitchen and dining room, where the destruction was equally thorough. The glass doors of the china cabinet had been smashed, the china and crystal torn from the shelves and tossed around the room. The banquet-size dining table had been hacked to pieces and the matching chairs smashed against the walls until they'd broken like matchsticks.

In the master bedroom, the new furniture he'd been waiting for with such impatience lay in pieces, completely destroyed. The mattress had been slashed, torn and shredded, the headboard shattered, the frame broken. The sledgehammer used in the attack lay nearby. On the wall, someone had sprayed in neon pink paint the words, "Back off, lawyer."

"Oh, Cam." Summer found him standing in the middle of the room, hands fisted at his sides, eyes narrowed on the paint-streaked wall.

She had to choke back a sob as she walked up behind him to wrap her arms around his waist and press her face to his shoulder. "Your beautiful new house."

He remained perfectly still for several minutes before turning her into his arms and pressing his lips to her temple. His words were muffled against her hair. "It's just a house, Summer. These are just things."

"But it's so senseless. So violent."

"Yeah." Violent enough to have his complete attention. Violent enough to let him know that the one responsible was capable of utter, total destruction.

This was neither random nor harmless. It could never be dismissed as the work of vandals or hoodlums. This was deliberate. Explosive. Calculated.

He held her another minute, needing her calm, steadying influence on the anger that had his blood heating to a boil.

When he was able to compose himself he took her hand. "Come on."

"Aren't you going to call the police?"

"Yeah. From my car phone. I need to breathe fresh air."

The police had been efficient, thorough, direct. After the inevitable questions, statements

and written reports, they had agreed to permit
Cam and Summer to leave while an investiga-
tion team continued going over the house and
grounds for any clues.

Cam dropped an arm around her shoulders as
he urged her toward his car. Once inside he
turned the key in the ignition and drove away
without a backward glance.

When they were on the highway she turned to
him. "I don't understand how you can simply
walk away."

"I'm not walking. I'm driving."

"This isn't funny, Cam. You know who did
this. Alfonso Johnson's signature is all over this.
You said yourself he was ready to erupt with
violence when you met with him. Yet you're
acting as though he's just one of many sus-
pects."

Cam's voice was dangerously soft. "I come
from a long line of cops, Summer. I know the
drill. I also know that a lot of things aren't what
they appear to be. Now let it go. What you need,
what we both need, is to find a way to work off
all this frustration."

"Please don't tell me you're driving us to a gym."

"I have a better idea. It's like a gym, but we'll manage to be surrounded by a little comfort, as well."

"Comfort?" She couldn't seem to follow his logic.

"I happen to know this place where the food is good, the atmosphere cozy and the company lively. And best of all, I can run, fight and sweat while enjoying it all."

She was shaking her head in disbelief. "How can you think about such things at a time like this?"

He merely continued driving until they'd returned to the city. When they came to a neighborhood of quiet streets, carefully tended lawns and big, sprawling houses, Cam slowed the car, then turned into a driveway where four cars were parked in a row.

"I'm not surprised." He turned off the ignition and sat a moment, looking at the blur of movement behind the front windows. "Looks like the gang's all here."

"The gang?"

He slid from the car and came around to open

her door. With her hand in his he led her up the steps and pushed open the front door.

"Shouldn't you knock?"

He smiled and led the way inside. "This is one place I never have to knock, Summer. The door is always open to me."

He saw understand dawning in her eyes and nodded. "This is where I grew up. Where I still come whenever I need to find sanity in an insane world. Welcome to my family home."

He leaned close and added, "Brace yourself. The Lassiter clan tends to be a bit overwhelming until you get to know them. Then they're just—" he gave her one of those quick, dangerous grins "—downright annoying."

Chapter 13

Kieran Lassiter looked up as they entered the kitchen.

Seeing Cam, a wide smile creased his face. "So, boyo. As usual you're here in time for supper. What's the matter? Wouldn't your favorite restaurant take your reservation?"

"Maybe I've maxed out my credit card."

"You, boyo? Not a chance. That fancy law firm pays you a king's ransom just to walk into court in those designer suits and dazzle the poor souls who have to sit and listen to you every day."

"You hear that?" Cam turned to Summer. "This is the sort of abuse I'm forced to endure in my own family."

In a loud voice he announced, "I'd like you all to meet Summer O'Connor. Summer, this is my grandfather, Kieran Lassiter."

Summer offered her hand. "Mr. Lassiter."

"It's plain old Pop." The old man caught her hand between both of his, staring into her eyes with a sly smile that reminded her of his grandson's. "Summer O'Connor, is it? That's a fine name."

"Thank you."

In his best brogue he asked, "You wouldn't happen to be related to Paddy O'Connor from County Cork now, would you?"

"That would be my grandfather, though I'm sure there are dozens more with the same name."

"A grand man, he was. A butcher, as I recall."

She shook her head. "My grandfather was a banker."

"A pity." He glanced at his daughter-in-law. "Have you met Cameron's mother, Kate?"

"I have."

Kate embraced her son before turning to Summer with a gentle smile. "Micah told us about the threatening message on your phone machine. I'm glad Cameron brought you here. This is my oldest son, Micah, and his wife, Pru."

Summer could see the resemblance between Cam and his older brother, especially in those midnight-blue eyes.

"My son Donovan and his wife, Andi, and their children Cory and Taylor."

Summer smiled and was rewarded by shy smiles from the children and warm handshakes from their parents.

Cam turned to include the handsome young couple standing by the big trestle table. "My sister, Bren, and her husband, Chris Banning."

Summer smiled at the tiny red-haired woman who looked like a younger version of Kate. "I've seen you on television, Congresswoman."

"It's just plain Bren."

"Bren." Summer offered her hand. "Chris." She looked around with a laugh. "I'm afraid it's going to take a while before I commit all of these names to memory."

"That's all right. Take your time." Donovan winked at Cam. "We'll wait until after dinner to give you the quiz."

Kieran chuckled. "I hope you've brought your appetite, lass. We're cooking a fine big meal."

Summer smiled almost shyly. "Something smells wonderful."

"It's pot roast. With mushroom gravy and new garden potatoes. And I'm baking biscuits. Dinner should be ready within the hour, if you've a mind to stay." He stared pointedly at his grandson and could see something hot and dangerous in those eyes. Something simmering just beneath the calm surface. "You are planning on staying, aren't you, boyo?"

"You bet." Cam nodded toward the battered old basketball hoop hanging over the garage in the back yard. "I've got a powerful need to beat up on something." He headed toward the back door. "I think there's just enough time before dinner to take on a couple of bloated old men." He turned to his brother-in-law. "Are you with me, Chris?"

"I'm your man." Chris discarded his jacket and rolled the sleeves of his police-issue shirt.

Micah turned to Donovan. "Who's this punk calling bloated?"

"You, bro."

At Donovan's laugh Micah taunted, "Then you must be the one he called old." He slapped his brother on the back. "Come on. Let's show our baby brother what we're made of."

The two men were out the door and racing after Cam and Chris, who were dribbling a basketball between them.

Summer stood in the bay window watching as they pushed, shoved and elbowed their way toward the basket. Micah went down on his knees, and Donovan jumped over him, shoving Cam against the backboard hard enough to have it swaying.

Summer turned to Pru and Andi, who had returned their attention to the stove. "Doesn't anyone mind that there are four men out there trying to hurt each other?"

"Don't give it a thought." Bren was busy tossing a salad. "They've been acting that way since they were out of diapers."

"You ought to know, lass." Kieran opened the oven to remove perfectly browned biscuits. "You've joined them too many times to count."

When he saw the look of alarm on Summer's face he walked over to draw an arm around her shoulders. "You're not to worry now. They might lose a little blood and rattle a few teeth, but they'll make it up before the game ends. The lads have always shot hoops whenever they needed to work off some energy. I'd say, by the anger I saw in Cameron's eyes when he first got here, he had a powerful need to shoot hoops with his brothers.''

When Summer remained silent he said, "Want to tell me what this is about?''

She shook her head. "I'll leave that up to Cam.''

"All right.'' He patted her hand. "Why don't you sit at the table and I'll make you a cup of tea.''

"I don't want you waiting on me. I'd like to help.''

He nodded. "All right. There are potatoes to mash and gravy to stir. Which will it be?''

She thought a minute, then rolled up her sleeves. Cam wasn't the only one who needed to work off some frustration. "I'll mash the potatoes.''

Kieran turned to the others, who were watching in silence. "Don't everybody just stand there. There's work to be done.''

Kate retrieved her oven mitts and lifted a

roasting pan from the oven. At the stove Andi began stirring gravy while Pru strained water from fresh garden beans. Kieran was filling a teapot with boiling water while Cory and Taylor were given the chore of carrying butter, cream and sugar to the dining room.

It was, Summer thought as she immersed herself in her chore, a very satisfying way of putting her worries aside.

"Here, boyo." Kieran handed Cam a bottle of chilled white wine.

The four men had worked up a healthy sweat and, except for Micah's bloody nose and Donovan's twisted ankle, seemed none the worse for the hour of combat. They were, in fact, looking very pleased with themselves.

"Make yourself useful."

With a wink at Summer the old man went back to his biscuits, arranging them in a napkin-lined basket.

When the wine was uncorked, Cam caught Summer's hand. "Come on. You can help me in the other room."

Once they were in the dining room he handed her the bottle before removing stem glasses from the china cabinet. While he held them, she poured. When the glasses had been filled and set around the table, he took the empty bottle from her hand and drew her close for a quick kiss.

At that exact moment Kieran stepped through the doorway and came to a sudden halt.

"We'll have none of that, boyo."

"Maybe you won't, Pop. Personally, I can't think of a better appetizer."

Though Summer's cheeks turned a becoming shade of pink, Cam merely laughed as the rest of his family spilled into the dining room behind Kieran.

They took their places around the table, with Kate at one end and Kieran at the other. Cam pulled a chair beside his for Summer, then took her hand in his. She glanced around the table to see that everyone had joined hands.

Kieran intoned the blessing in his rich, deep voice. "Bless this food and those who are about to enjoy it. Bless our guest this evening, and make her feel at home. And especially bless Riordan who watches over us all."

Summer glanced at Cam and saw the slight flare of his nostrils at the mention of his father. It seemed amazing to her that this family had kept one man alive in their memories, even though they'd been little more than children when he'd died.

As they began passing dishes, they all seemed to be talking at once.

"So, Summer." Micah offered her the basket of biscuits. "What do you do?"

She set a perfectly browned biscuit on her plate and passed the basket to Cam. "I'm a social worker."

Bren looked across the table. "Do you work with Mom?"

"No. But we've met. Everyone in our department has great respect for Kate Lassiter."

At the end of the table Kate merely smiled. "Ours is a mutual admiration society. We're probably the only ones who know how difficult and frustrating the job can be. Pru does similar work at the Children's Village."

Summer angled her head. "I'm impressed. I've dealt with Children's Village from time to time. They handle even difficult family cases with ease."

Pru acknowledged the compliment with a smile. "Actually, I don't work with the families, but rather with the computers."

Donovan sipped his wine. "How'd you happen to meet Cameron?"

Summer glanced at Cam. "We found ourselves on opposite sides of a current case."

Chris grinned at his wife. "Not a bad way to get acquainted. That's pretty much how Bren and I met."

"Really?" Summer lifted a brow.

Bren was laughing. "We appeared on 'Meet the Media' to debate opposite sides of an issue."

Chris closed his hand over his wife's. "And found ourselves agreeing more often than disagreeing."

Cam made a mock gagging sound. "You'll have to forgive the newlyweds. With them around, we don't need sugar in our tea."

"Jealous?" Bren shot him a look. "I'm sure to a hard-core bachelor like you, the thought of two people pledging their love forever must seem so dull."

"Mary Brendan." Kieran's tone was sharp. "Another outburst like that, and you'll find yourself out back shooting hoops."

Cam couldn't help laughing. In an aside he whispered, "Some things never change. From the time we were kids, whenever we got out of hand, Pop sent us outside to work off our frustrations playing basketball.''

Summer's eyes widened. ''But your sister is a Congresswoman, for heaven sake. You don't mean he can still order her outside?''

''He can and does. In the Lassiter house, Pop rules. Whatever he says, we do.''

Summer muttered, ''I wonder what he'd have done with Elise.''

''He'd have turned your sister into a proper young lady with an admirable work ethic, or she'd have found a career on a professional women's basketball team.''

The two of them were laughing as the meal wore on and the conversation swirled around them.

''So, this case you're working on.'' Donovan speared another slice of beef from the platter and winked at his wife. ''Are the two of you still on opposite sides?''

Summer shook her head, hoping no one would notice her lack of appetite. The threatening message on her phone and the destruction of Cam's house had her more shaken than she cared to admit. ''I think it's safe to say we agree more than we disagree.''

"Very smart, little bro." Micah glanced at his grandfather. "Before I take a second helping, I'd like to know what you've planned for dessert."

The old man was grinning. "Hot apple strudel with caramel ice cream."

Micah shook his head. "Now that's some serious dessert. I guess I'll forget about seconds."

"Me, too." Little Taylor drained her glass of milk and started to wipe her mouth on her sleeve until she caught the look her mother gave her. Then she reached for her napkin. "Can I help serve it, Pop?"

"You bet." Kieran pushed away from the table. "Come on, sweetheart. The ones who serve always get the biggest slices."

"Can I help, too?" Cory called.

"Too late." Donovan tousled the boy's hair. "In this family you've got to be on your toes if you want to be first."

They were still laughing when Kieran and Taylor began passing around the plates of strudel, still warm from the oven, topped with caramel ice cream.

While they served the dessert, Kate circled the table filling teacups. As she reached for Summer's plate she touched a hand to the young woman's shoulder and whispered, "Are you all right, dear?"

"Yes. Thank you." Summer felt oddly comforted by the touch of Kate's hand as she squeezed gently before moving on.

Micah dug into his dessert. "Do you remember the time Dad decided to make dinner because Mom was sick in bed? He put so much pasta in the pot it boiled up all over the stove."

Donovan nodded. "How could I forget? I got the job of cleaning up that lovely mess."

Bren chuckled. "Then he got the bright idea of making corned beef hash. We took one taste and called it Alpo. Dad got so mad he packed us into his squad car and took us down to the corner diner."

Micah shook his head. "Burned hot dogs and greasy fries never tasted so good."

That had everyone roaring with laughter.

Summer sat back, sipping tea and listening. Kieran was already leaping to the defense of his son, while Kate was reminding her children that their father always did his best.

Summer glanced at Cam. Did he remember this event, as the others did? Or had he merely heard the story so many times, he thought he remembered it?

Though her heart ached for him, and for the father he'd lost when he was just a boy, she thought how lucky he was to have such a loving, caring family. Riordan Lassiter seemed as much a part of this family now as when he'd been here in their midst.

Perhaps, she realized with sudden clarity, it was because he was still here with them. They'd kept his memory alive all these years so that he could remain the father they needed. The leader they followed. The hero they admired.

Summer noted the sudden lull in the conversation and realized someone had asked her a question. She gave a start. "I'm sorry. I guess I was drifting."

"That's all right." Andi glanced at her son and daughter. "Why don't we clear the table and load the dishwasher."

"I'll help." As Summer started to push away from the table Andi lay a hand on hers. "No. You need to stay and talk. The children and I can handle this."

As soon as the table was cleared and the children gone, Micah broke the silence. "So. You received a threatening message on your phone machine.''

Summer nodded. ''Cam said he asked you to see about taking extra security measures at my apartment.''

''It's already in place.'' He turned to his younger brother. ''Okay. Now it's time you filled us in on the rest.''

''How do you know there's more?''

''For one thing, you had a look of murder in your eye when you first got here. For another, that was one of the roughest games you've played in years. I'd say that all adds up to something bigger than a threatening message on a telephone. So, what gives?''

Cam glanced at his mother, wishing he could spare her. ''We went to my place, intending to spend the night there. It's been trashed.''

''Cameron.'' Kate clamped a hand over her mouth. ''Your new home?''

He frowned. ''The caller left an interesting message on my bedroom wall.''

Chris asked softly, ''Did you notify the police?''

''Yeah. Chief Newberg promised to call you

as soon as he knew anything conclusive. I hope you don't mind that I gave him your name.''

Bren's husband was already on his feet. ''I'll just call him now and see what they've come up with.''

Cam gave a grim smile. ''Thanks, Chris. I figured you'd handle it for me.''

Minutes later Chris returned to say, ''Chief Newberg is faxing me his report. He's a good cop, Cam. And a thorough one. He said he's assigned his best men to the case.''

''That's good news, Chris. Thanks.'' Cam turned to his mother. ''I'm hoping Summer and I can stay here tonight.''

''You know you're both welcome.'' Kate gave Summer a gentle smile. ''You can have Bren's old room.''

Bren added, ''As the only rose among all these thorns, I was given an adjoining bathroom.''

Summer was already shaking her head in protest as she got to her feet. ''I don't want to be any trouble. I can go to my parents' house in Georgetown.''

''They're out of town. You'd be alone.'' Cam

closed his hands over her upper arms. "I'd feel better knowing you were safe here."

Aware of his family, she put aside a desire to touch a hand to his cheek and merely nodded. "All right. I'll sleep better knowing I'm not alone."

"That's my girl." Keeping one arm around her waist, he turned to Chris. "How soon do you expect that fax?"

"It should come through my department soon. I'll have my assistant notify me as soon as it arrives."

From her position across the room Kate Lassiter studied her son and the young woman beside him and absorbed a jolt at the realization that they had become, in the space of weeks, much more than friends.

She glanced at her father-in-law and knew, by the way he was watching, that he'd sensed it, as well.

She sighed as the rest of her children prepared to take their leave. And wondered when her youngest son had grown into such a strong, determined man.

And so like his father it was like looking at a scene from the past.

Chapter 14

"Bren always loved this room. I think you'll be comfortable here." Kate stood in the doorway and watched as Summer looked around.

"I'm sure I will be. Thank you, Kate. This is very generous of you."

"Not at all. I'm happy to have you here. I just wish it had been under happier circumstances. Have you told your parents?"

Summer shook her head. "I'd hate to dump this on them when they're out of the country and helpless to do anything about it. I'm hoping by the time they return, the police will have found whoever is responsible."

Kate took a step closer. "Cam said both incidents seemed to point to Alfonso Johnson as the one who planned them."

"It looks that way. I'm sorry, Kate. I know you were hoping to reunite him with his son."

"I wonder..." With a shrug, Kate turned away.

"You wonder what?" With a hand to her arm Summer stopped her.

Kate turned back. "I wonder why he would jeopardize his best, and perhaps his only, chance for a new trial by doing something so reckless?"

"Maybe he learned that his wife is seeking custody of his son and he wants to show her that even behind bars, he isn't helpless."

Kate shrugged. "Maybe. But I'm sure you know, as Tio's caseworker, that if Alfonso were to be found not guilty, he would stand as much chance of obtaining custody of Tio as the mother who abandoned him."

"He might. If my recommendations should lean in his direction. After all that's happened, his chances grow slimmer by the day."

"My point exactly." Kate turned away and paced to the window, arms crossed over her chest.

"You think someone's setting it up to make him look guilty?"

Kate shook her head. "I wish I knew."

Watching her, Summer impulsively asked, "Would you mind if I asked you something?" When Kate merely smiled she asked, "What led you into the work you've chosen?"

Kate leaned a hip against the sill. "I think it was seeing the devastation in my family when Riordan died." She pointed to a framed photo of a handsome young police officer who bore a striking resemblance to Cam.

While Summer walked to the desk to study the photo, Kate said, "It made me understand just how important, and how fragile, family really is." She paused a moment before saying, "It's strange how one event can change everything. If Riordan had lived, I'm sure I'd have gone on, complacently raising my family, living the life I'd envisioned for myself. My children, too, would have been different. Their father was a strong man. Maybe, had he lived, they'd have learned to lean on him. With him gone, they had to dig deep and find their own strengths." She looked up as Summer turned. "Strange. I never stopped to analyze my motives." She smiled.

''Good night, Summer. If you need anything at all, please let me know.''

''Thank you. And Kate, if it's any comfort, I hope you're right about Alfonso Johnson. I'd really like it to be anyone but him responsible for all this.''

When she was alone Summer undressed, then climbed into the tidy bed and lay watching the play of moonlight filtering through the part in the curtains.

Odd. She'd meant what she'd said to Kate. Even though she'd been initially against Tio having any contact with his father in prison and had made her feelings clear to her superiors, she'd experienced a gradual change of heart. And most of it was because of Cam.

It had been a revelation seeing him with his family. Despite the teasing and good-natured banter, there was a deep well of love here. So much support for one another. Maybe it was as Kate said. Having lost their father while still very young, they took greater care of such feelings.

Some of Cam's tension had eased once he'd returned to his home. Still, she couldn't help noticing how tired he'd looked as the night wore on. He was very good at making his job look easy, even though she knew better. It wasn't possible to attain the status of top lawyer at a competitive firm like Stern Hayes Wheatley without being married to the job.

Married to the job.

Wasn't that what her sister had accused her of, when she'd declined the opportunity to go to Europe? And it had been true. Her work had become the most important thing to her.

Until Cameron Lassiter had entered her life.

Maybe *entered* was too mild a term. He'd blown in like a storm and had completely taken over her life. And now, though she was afraid to probe too deeply, their lives had become entangled. Like those lovely vinca vines she'd planted in the containers on her balcony. Curled around each other, unable to tell where one began and the other ended.

How had this happened? How had she let it go this far?

She'd tried to deny the initial attraction. She'd always avoided smooth, handsome men. Maybe because they'd always been more attracted to her sister. Elise was the pretty one. Summer had heard that from her mother all her life. And she'd been called the smart one. Funny how those labels, lightly applied in childhood, carried over into adult lives. She'd always been considered the odd one in her family. Too serious. And never quite fitting in with their lavish lifestyle. She'd chosen textbooks over art classes. Youth hostels over spas. Working at children's camps rather than touring Europe with her mother and sister.

Not that she hadn't had her share of fun and laughter and boyfriends. But she'd made a habit of dodging serious entanglements, leaving those for her starry-eyed sister, while she'd doggedly pursued a career. Ever the idealist, she deliberately chose something that she hoped would make a difference. She cared about the people who came to the state agency for help, feeling lost, confused, desperate. She liked to think that because of her concern, at least a few lives were better.

When she'd entered into social work she hadn't expected it to be a smooth ride. But she'd never dreamed she might find her safety, and that of the man she loved, threatened.

The man she loved.

She sat up, running her hands through her hair. Where had such a thought come from?

Restless, she got out of bed and pulled on a silk kimono before stepping into the hallway. The bedroom doors were closed, with no light showing beneath them. She descended the stairs and followed a faint trail of light to the kitchen.

Kieran was standing with his back to her, staring out the bay window into the darkness. A sliver of moonlight cast a bronze tint on his white hair. In his hand was a cup. Steam drifted toward the ceiling.

Hearing her footsteps he turned. "Can't sleep, lass?"

Summer shook her head. "Too much excitement, I guess."

"Join me for some tea, then." Kieran retrieved another cup and saucer. "Cream and sugar?"

She shook her head. "Just black, thanks."

She accepted the cup from his hands and settled herself at the trestle table. After one sip she felt her tensions ease. There was something about this big bear of a man, a quiet strength that made her feel as though she'd reached a safe haven in a storm.

"Cam told me how you came to live with his family after the death of his father."

Kieran settled himself beside her. "It was a turbulent time for all of us."

"They were lucky to have you."

"I was the lucky one, lass. Riordan was my only child. I'd have rather had my heart cut out of me than go through the pain of that loss. I had no reason left to live. Kate and the children gave me a reason."

"I'm sure you've given back just as much through the years."

He shook his head. "I could never repay them for what they've given me. How can a man put a value on his life? I was dead the day I buried my son. Convinced I wouldn't live to see another morning. And then, somehow, through my tears I saw their need. And it was greater than mine."

He went very still for a moment, as though turning inward. Then he gave her a steady look. "I don't think you came down here to talk about me."

She looked at her tea. "I'm afraid."

"You've a right to be. The message left on your machine was a threat."

She shook her head. "I don't mean about me, although I am uneasy. I mean about Cam. I saw something...a fierceness in his eyes that frightened me. I'm afraid he'll do something foolish. Something reckless."

"Ah." He spoke the word on a long sigh.

She looked up. "Can't you convince him to step back and let the police do their job?"

He sat back with a strange smile playing on his lips. "Careful, lass. People hearing you right now might think you're beginning to care about him a bit too much."

"Of course I..." For just a moment she was caught off guard. Then she gave a low, throaty laugh. "You're a very sly man, Kieran Lassiter."

"So I've been told." His smile deepened. "Funny. I had much this same discussion with my grandson just an hour ago."

"You did?"

He nodded. "Cameron is deeply troubled. He asked me to find a way to keep you close until this business is settled. He seems to think you're a rare treasure that needs protecting."

She sipped tea to hide her pleasure at his words.

Seeing it, the old man lay a hand over hers. "We can't help worrying over the ones we love. It's been the way of it from the beginning of time. But I'll tell you this about Cameron. He's a scrapper. Always was. I could see, almost from the time he was born, that he was the most like his father. Perhaps that's why I fought so hard to help him channel all that restless energy. All that heat simmering inside him, ready to ignite. I'd lost Riordan. I couldn't bear to lose the one made in his image. I'd made mistakes with the father. I believed I was given a second chance with the son."

"I don't understand."

Kieran sipped his tea. Thought awhile. "Some men are born to fight, lass. It's in their blood. But there are other ways to fight than with fists or guns. Unlike his father, Cameron was also blessed with an outstanding mind. That's his weapon. He uses it well. And even if he should find himself engaged in a street brawl with thugs and bullies, he has the advantage of that brain."

"It won't stop a bullet."

He shook his head. "That it won't. As his father learned all too well. But maybe it can prevent the bullet from being fired in the first place.''

Summer sighed. ''I hope you're right, Pop.''

At her easy use of his nickname the old man smiled. ''You're beginning to sound like one of the family, lass.''

''It's a bit early for that. Cam and I have only known each other a few weeks.''

''Sometimes all it takes is one minute.'' His smile grew pensive, and he got up, restless, to stare once more out the window. ''I knew, the first time I saw Margaret Doyle dancing with my best friend, that she would one day be my wife.''

''How long were you married?''

He didn't turn around. ''Not long enough, lass. Not nearly long enough. I still miss her every day. Just as I miss my son.''

Summer set her cup and saucer in the dishwasher, then walked over to stand behind him. She touched a hand lightly to his shoulder. ''Good night, Pop. Thanks for the tea.''

He patted her hand. ''Thanks for the company. It was just what I needed tonight.''

Summer left him alone with his memories.

As she climbed the stairs, it occurred to her that this was a house filled with memories.

Maybe that was why she felt so comfortable here.

Or maybe it was simply because of the man asleep in the upper apartment.

Whatever the reason, she felt more at home here, with Cam's family, than she did with her own. Maybe because this was a cohesive, unified family, while her own had been four individuals sharing the same address. Though her life had been sprinkled with exotic travel and cushioned with fine art, she'd always felt a yearning for something simpler. Until now she hadn't recognized what her heart had sought. Home. Family. And the pleasures of sharing.

Using the moonlight as her guide she let herself into Bren's old room and slid into bed, then let out a gasp as the mattress sagged under the weight of another.

"Cam." His name came out on a whoosh of air.

"Sorry." He pressed his lips to her cheek, sending heat curling along her spine. "I didn't mean to scare you. What were you and Pop talking about for so long?"

She snuggled into the circle of his arms, feeling the last of her worries dissolve. With her mouth to his she whispered, "Fighters. And lovers."

"Really?" He ran wet, nibbling kisses along the soft column of her throat, feeling the need for her, sharp as a knife, slice through him. "Which am I?"

She felt herself sinking into that soft, warm cocoon he always managed to spin around them. "I think I'm about to find out."

Hearing voices downstairs, Summer showered and dressed quickly before descending the stairs. When she stepped into the kitchen, she found Kate seated at the table, calmly eating, while Cam was carrying on a heated argument with his grandfather.

"I don't have time for eggs and sausage, Pop. I've got a call in to the firm to see what they've decided to do about the McGonnagle-Carlson case. Everything hinges on whether or not we go to trial. On top of that I'm expecting a report from Chief Newberg on what they found out at my place. And I'm about to phone Tio's grandmother to see if I can take the boy up to the prison today to talk to his dad."

"All the more reason you need fuel, boyo."

Without missing a beat Kieran continued turning eggs in a skillet.

Summer paused in mid-stride. "After all the days Tio's missed, you'd take that boy out of school again?"

Cam could hear the disapproval in her tone. "Since this involves him and his father, they have a right to know what's going on. I'm hoping Alfonso can shed some light on this matter."

"Why would he? If he's guilty, he'd be incriminating himself. If he isn't, why should a convict care what goes on outside his cell?"

"Think about it, Summer. These threats were designed to make Alfonso Johnson look like he can still pull strings while serving time, like some mob boss or gang leader. I've begun to believe that he doesn't come close to fitting either image. I believe he cares deeply about his son. If that's true, and someone else is orchestrating all this, Alfonso has to feel frustrated knowing he can't be there to protect his family."

"What about you? And us?" She deliberately kept her voice low, to hide her conflicting feelings. Even while she feared for him, she felt a flash of annoyance that he hadn't said a word to her about his plan to visit Alfonso again until now. "Who's going to protect you, Cam, if you persist in this?"

He closed a hand over hers. "Don't worry about me. I'll be fine. As for you, that's why you're here. Pop promised to stick close to you until this thing is resolved."

Her eyes narrowed fractionally. "You don't really think I'm going to just stay here locked safely away and allow myself to be...baby-sat while you're going about your routine."

"Yeah. I do."

She put her hands on her hips. "If you're going to take Tio to see his father, I'm going with you."

"Why would you do that? You know you can't stand the thought of going up there."

"That's right. I can't. But Tio is my responsibility. And I intend to see to him. I've already alerted my supervisors to the threat that's been made. Now I'll let them know that I'm accompanying the boy to prison to see his father."

Cam was already shaking his head. "I won't have you—"

"You can't stop me. Besides, without my approval in this, Tio will have to repeat his grade again next year. Do you want that?"

Cam sighed in defeat. He knew, by the sparks in those eyes, that she meant business. "All right. Call your superiors and explain. I'll phone Tio's grandmother and make arrangements to pick him up there."

As Summer reached for her cell phone, Cam huffed out a breath and watched his grandfather set down two plates heaped with scrambled eggs, sausages and toast, followed with tall glasses of orange juice. "It seems while you and I were momentarily distracted, Pop wasted no time winning his argument by default."

Across the table Kate merely grinned. "This same argument has been going on since you were five, Cameron. I don't know why you should think you'd win now."

He gave a sigh of disgust before settling himself at the table beside Summer.

As he dug into the mountain of food he said, "This is why all the Lassiters work so hard. Otherwise our arteries would get so clogged, we'd be moving at a snail's pace."

Kieran filled coffee cups, then sat at the table with his own breakfast. "Eggs have been getting a bad rap, boyo. They're a natural source of protein."

Cam winked at Summer. "You'd think he owned stock in chicken farms."

The old man merely grinned. "Who's to say I don't?"

Chapter 15

Summer sat on one side of the metal table, holding her hands in her lap to hide the fact that they were trembling. She couldn't help remembering her first and only visit here, when Alfonso Johnson had ordered her out. There had been such hatred and loathing in his eyes when he'd learned her reason for the visit. No one, he'd shouted, had the right to take his son from him.

Now she was back, trusting that Cam was right in this matter. But a part of her was terrified that all the rage bottled up inside this prisoner would simply explode.

She knew there was a guard outside the door and a panic button on the wall to her left. Still, she couldn't help wondering how long it would take to push the button and get the guard to react if anything went wrong. She could imagine a man as violent as Alfonso Johnson reaching across the table and grabbing her by the throat, choking the life out of her before she could be saved.

She felt a hand close over hers and looked up in time to see Cam wink.

Taking a deep breath, she forced herself to relax.

The door opened, and Alfonso Johnson was escorted into the room. As he took a seat at the table his dark gaze flicked over his son, then narrowed on Summer and Cam before returning to the boy.

"How you doing, Tio?"

"Good."

"How's school?"

"Okay."

"You going to be held back because of this visit?"

The boy shook his head. "Miss O'Connor fixed it with the teacher."

Alfonso turned an angry look on Summer. "Why are you meddling?"

Before she could speak Cam interrupted. "We needed to talk to you and figured, since we were coming out here, you'd enjoy a visit with Tio."

"Talk to me about what?" The man fixed that cold stare on Cam.

"Someone's gone to a lot of trouble to get our attention. You know anything about it?"

"Why don't you tell me about it."

"Threats were left on Summer's phone. My home was trashed. Someone went to a great deal of trouble to blame you."

Alfonso shrugged. "Wouldn't be the first time."

Cam's tone went deadly soft. "It had better be the last."

"You threatening me, law boy? You think, because you're the expert here, you can hurt me worse than I've been hurt? Look around you. The law took away my freedom. Took away my name. But nobody..." He lowered his voice for emphasis. "Nobody is going to take away my boy. Especially no lying female who's trying to pin this rap on me."

"Are you saying you know who's behind this?"

"Same one's been behind every bad thing ever happened in my life. A man loses his heart to the wrong woman, he's going to pay, big time." Alfonso glanced at his son, then, seeing the pain in the boy's eyes, clamped his mouth shut and shoved back his chair. "I got nothing more to say. Sorry you came all this way for nothing."

"It wasn't for nothing." Cam stood, as well, and seeing the boy's shoulders droop in defeat, lay a hand gently on his arm. "There's nothing worse than a son being separated from his father." He looked up, staring into those world-weary eyes. "That's something else I'm an expert on."

Something flickered in Alfonso's eyes before he turned away. In this place, everybody knew about the hard-eyed lawyer whose police-officer father had taken a bullet for his partner.

Seconds later the door opened. In tight-lipped silence Alfonso was escorted to his cell, while Summer and Cam walked to the visitor's entrance with Tio between them.

* * *

Cam glanced in the rearview mirror. Despite Summer's attempts at conversation, Tio hadn't spoken a word since leaving prison.

"I figure, since we've already blown off half the school day, we may as well take the rest of it, as well. How about some lunch?"

In silence Tio turned his head and stared out the side window.

Summer made an attempt at a smile. It had been harder than she'd expected, watching the father and son together. Though they'd been separated by mere inches, the width of a narrow table, it may as well have been miles. There was no loving embrace. No goodbye kiss. The coldness of it, the harshness of it, had left her heart aching for man and boy.

But despite any lack of public affection, there was a bond there. A thread that prison walls and years of separation couldn't break. Shouldn't break.

She forced a lightness to her voice she didn't feel. "Lunch sounds good."

"There's a place a few miles up the highway. Tio and I stopped there last time." Cam turned his head slightly. "Remember?"

The boy ignored him, choosing to look away.

With a sigh Cam returned his attention to the road. As he did, he caught sight of a silver truck parked along the shoulder. When he drew alongside, the truck suddenly swerved onto the highway. It was only Cam's quick thinking that saved them from impact.

"Crazy driver." He glanced in the rearview mirror to find the truck coming up behind them at breakneck speed. As he shouted a warning the truck hit the rear of Cam's sports car, sending it veering across the grassy median, into oncoming traffic.

Cam gripped the wheel and managed to steer between cars, the drivers looking terrified as they sped around and past him on either side. When there was a break in traffic he pulled to the side of the road, where the car came to a shuddering halt.

"Are you all right?" He leaned over to touch a hand to Summer's.

"I'm...fine." She struggled to catch a breath through a throat that had been clogged with panic.

"Tio?"

In the back seat the boy was white-knuckling the door handle, too terrified to speak.

Summer drew in a shaky breath. "That was no accident."

Cam's eyes narrowed with concentration. "I know." He tossed her his cell phone. "Call the police."

Just as Summer began dialing, Cam looked up to catch a flash of silver out of the corner of his eye. The truck had hit the brakes and spun in a half circle before driving across the median straight toward them.

Cam stomped on the gas, desperate to return to the other side of the highway before there was any more traffic to bar his escape. The car bumped across a grassy mound, slammed onto the highway and took off at high speed with the truck in hot pursuit.

If they were on a racetrack, Cam had no doubt he could outrun the truck. His little sports car would leave that vehicle in its dust. But this was a busy highway in the middle of a workday. Ahead were cars meandering in both lanes, blocking his escape. As he came up behind the first line of cars and began to slow down, he could see the truck speeding up.

Again he shouted a warning. When he felt the impact he had to grip the wheel with all his strength to stay on course and keep from hitting the car in front of him.

When there was another break in traffic he sped up and swerved between two cars. Behind him the truck stayed doggedly on his tail, nipping at his bumper, sending the little car swaying from lane to lane.

Cam looked at the miles of concrete looming ahead of them. In the distance he could see the cloverleaf leading to overhead ramps for exits and entrances. All around them were cars filled with drivers and passengers. Though he was desperate to save Summer and Tio, he knew he had to do it without doing harm to innocent bystanders.

He glanced in the rearview mirror, his eyes narrowing with sudden determination. The lessons learned so long ago were never far from his mind. Since he couldn't avoid the inevitable, he'd play it smart.

"Okay," he muttered aloud. "You want to fight? Fine. But you'll do it on my terms."

At the next break in traffic he hit the accelerator, and the little car shot ahead. The truck sped up but even at top speed couldn't catch them until they were forced to slow down behind a stream of cars.

Threading his way between them, Cam struggled to stay on track when they were once again hit from behind. When he skidded off the highway, his wheels spewing dirt, the truck was right behind him, bumping him again and again. He managed to get the car onto the highway, and they shot ahead, the truck fighting to keep up.

Cam kept just ahead of the truck until he caught another break in traffic. Then he veered sharply right, toward the ramp leading to the highway exit.

Sensing that he was about to get away, the truck's driver accelerated. With a mighty roar of engine he barreled up behind Cam's car, determined to drive it into the concrete wall.

As he headed toward the wall of concrete, Cam heard Summer's scream. He wanted desperately to soothe her. To comfort her. More than anything, to tell her that he loved her. But he needed to focus all his concentration on what he was about to do.

With the truck hugging his bumper he struggled to hold the wheel steady as the concrete loomed ahead of him. At the last moment, with split-second timing, he turned the wheel, and the little car shot up the ramp.

Behind him there was a terrible explosion as the truck smashed head-on into the retaining wall.

Cam managed to bring his car to a shuddering stop on the shoulder, where he sat perfectly silent, feeling the steering wheel still vibrating in his hands. They'd come so close. So perilously close to death.

For the longest time they sat without moving, without speaking, as they struggled with a mixture of fear and dread and relief.

It didn't seem possible for anyone to survive such a crash. But as Summer turned to look, she saw a figure crawling from the wreckage.

"Cam. There's someone back there."

She released her seat belt. On trembling legs she stepped from the car. Cam and Tio joined her, and the three of them raced to the fiery vehicle, where someone was struggling to free the driver.

As they arrived, fingers of fire shot out, sending the figure stumbling backward. Flames engulfed the wreckage, trapping the driver inside.

The one who'd been fighting to free him

caught sight of them and pulled out a handgun. "You killed him."

They froze. Though it was impossible to tell, through the blood and smoke, who this survivor was, the voice was unmistakably female.

"He killed himself with his reckless behavior." Cam carefully stepped in front of Summer and Tio, shielding their bodies with his.

He groaned in silent protest when Summer stepped beside him and confronted the woman. "Why were you trying to kill us? Did Alfonso send you?"

"Alfonso?" The woman gave a rasping laugh. "Oh, yeah. He sent us, all right. To hell and back." Her voice lowered with feeling. "The only place he'd send me is to one of those miserable detox centers. The only thing he was ever good for was preaching about living a good life while fetching garbage."

"Don't you talk about him like that." Tio started forward, his hands clenched into fists at his sides. "Don't you say another word about my dad."

"You little fool. When are you going to stop defending him? I'm the one gave you life."

Summer stared in absolute disbelief. "You're... Jobina Johnson? Tio's mother?"

"Yeah. And I know you. You're Goody Two-shoes. The one who was supposed to get me custody. But all you did was shuffle papers. Galt warned me I'd never get custody." She waved the pistol at Tio. "Get over here, boy."

Before he could obey Cam caught him by the wrist and drew him behind him. "You can't have him."

"Who's going to stop me? You?" Jobina swayed slightly and gave a high, shrill laugh that had the hair at the back of Summer's neck bristling.

In an aside Cam whispered, "Take the boy and run while I distract her."

Summer shook her head. "I'm not leaving you."

She watched as the woman took aim. "No!"

Even as she shouted a warning, the bullet ripped through Cam with such force, he clutched his chest and dropped to the grass.

Summer bent to him, stunned by the river of blood spilling down his shirt. Her eyes filled with tears, and she had to hold back the sob that rose up in her throat.

Cam was struggling to remain conscious. He had to. Or they'd all be lost. "For Tio's sake, Summer, run."

"I won't leave you." She could see Jobina's agitation growing.

The woman brandished the gun and drew closer, until Summer could smell the stench of liquor and see the glint of madness in her eyes.

She stood up, desperate to keep this woman's attention away from Cam. "Tell me something. If you knew Tio was in the car, why didn't you try to save him?"

"Save him? Why would I save his sorry hide? He's just like his old man."

Stunned, Summer could only gasp at the hatred spewing from this woman. "But if you wanted him dead, why do you want him now?"

The woman pointed with her gun. "Hear that?"

In the distance they could hear the shrill call of sirens gradually growing louder.

"He's my ticket out of here. And afterward, I'll do what I should have done a long time ago. It'll be my last parting gift to my good-for-nothing husband."

"Don't call him that." Tio's cry in defense of his father was like a knife in Summer's heart.

She held on to him tightly, determined not to let him go with this madwoman. "You'd kill the boy just to spite his father? Why do you hate Alfonso so?"

Jobina's eyes narrowed. "He never let me have any fun. All I ever heard was that I had to be better now that I had a kid. No drinking. No partying. If I'd known having a kid would change my life like that, I'd have never had him. I only did it so he'd marry me. But afterward he changed." She gave a smug smile. "That's why I set him up. My boyfriend Galt and I planned the whole thing. I sent Alfonso to the store that night. Galt did the rest."

"You set up your own husband?"

The woman laughed. "Do you know what it's like to be tied down with a kid and a man who'd rather collect garbage than have a good time? But even in prison, he wouldn't get out of my way. He had his mama fight for custody so I wouldn't have any money from the state. I hated him for that. Hated the old woman, too. So when Galt found out someone was sniffing around that old crime, he figured we could make it work in our favor by scaring the two of you off and maybe getting the kid in the bargain." She glared at the boy. "I don't want you, boy. I've never wanted you. But you were a meal ticket. Now I figure if I kill Alfonso's kid, I take away his reason for living. That'll teach him to mess with me."

Summer tried to breathe. The hatred coming from this woman seemed to roll over her in bitter, stifling waves. "The police are almost here." She knew it was a desperate plea, but she had no choice. "If you leave now, you might get away."

"Not without the kid."

"If you try to take Tio with you, you'll have to kill me first."

"You think I care about your miserable life?" Jobina gave an evil smile and took aim.

Shaking his head to clear his vision, Cam struggled to his knees. Pain rolled over him, threatening to take him down. He couldn't let it. If he'd ever thought himself a fighter, this was his chance to prove it.

It was a slim chance, but it was all he had. He prayed Summer would keep up the distraction.

As if reading his mind Summer said, "Remember this. Once you kill me, the police will never give up the hunt for you. The choice is yours. You can run now or stick around to finish me off and risk being caught."

Jobina's finger closed around the trigger. "I'll take my chances with the kid."

Cam sprang up, closing the distance between them and pouncing on the woman at the same moment she squeezed the trigger. The impact had the gun slipping from her fingers, landing in the grass a short distance away. Though she was drunk and dazed, Jobina fought like a caged tiger, her fingernails raking his face and teeth sinking into his arm.

Tio scrambled around them and snatched up the pistol. His eyes were hot and dry, his voice firm. "Stop now." He couldn't call her by name. Wouldn't give her the satisfaction. "You stop or I swear I'll use this."

"No!" Summer stepped in front of him, determined to shield him from doing something he would regret for a lifetime. She held out her hand. Though it was trembling violently, she took a step closer. "Tio, give me the gun."

''You heard her. She put my father in prison. She wants to kill all of us.''

''And she'll pay for that. But this isn't the way. Killing is never the way to even a score.'' Summer's heart was thundering so frantically, she was afraid it would leap right out of her chest. ''Give me the gun, Tio. Now.''

For the space of a heartbeat the boy seemed about to refuse. His head turned from side to side in denial.

''Think about all the things your father has suffered because of a gun, Tio. All the years he's missed with you and your grandmother. Don't let the same thing happen to you.''

The boy went very still, remembering all the things his father had told him about the evils of guns. He took in a long, deep breath, then placed the gun in Summer's hand.

Summer looked at it with disgust before tossing as far as she could. Then, hearing Cam's grunt of pain, she hurried over to take hold of Jobina's hair, yanking her away from Cam with such force, the woman let out a cry of pain.

Jobina turned on her with all the fury of a tornado, kicking, biting, scratching. In defense, Summer did something she'd have never thought possible. Closing her hand into a fist, she brought it against Jobina's jaw with such force, the woman dropped like a stone.

Summer turned to Cam, who sank to his knees in the grass.

Helping him to his feet, she wrapped her arms around his waist. "Oh, my darling. You're bleeding. Hold on to me."

"I'd...like that." He staggered slightly as he watched half a dozen police cars come to a screeching halt.

Within seconds uniformed men were swarming over the area.

Chris Banning hurried over, followed by an emergency medical team. As they lay Cam on a stretcher and began to probe his wound, Summer and Tio clung together, watching with matching looks of concern.

"Is he going to be all right?" Summer thought her heart would surely stop.

The medic looked up with a nod. "First bullet went clean through the fleshy part of his arm. Second one seems to have missed the vitals. Going to hurt like hell, but he'll be up and moving in no time."

At that, Summer burst into tears.

"Hey, now." Cam reached up, trying vainly to offer some comfort.

But now that the dam had burst, Summer was beyond soothing. Tears rolled down her cheeks, and she wiped at them with the backs of her hands. "Oh, Cam. I was so afraid you were going to die."

As she fell into his arms he gave her one of those cocky, heart-stopping smiles. "Not a chance."

"How could you be so sure?"

Over her head he winked at Tio. "You really ought to meet the Lassiters, boy. You're not the only one with a hard-as-nails dad who'll fight for you. Mine's got the strength of the angels on his side."

For the first time that he could remember, Cam saw Tio Johnson smile.

He could feel himself drifting, and knew it was only a matter of minutes before he'd lose consciousness. It seemed to him there were so many things he wanted to say to Summer.

But as police officers swarmed over the area, bagging the handgun for evidence and carrying the limp form of Jobina toward a squad car, all he managed to mutter was, "You know something, O'Connor? You pack a hell of a punch."

Epilogue

Chris Banning pulled the squad car up the driveway of the big, sprawling house and turned with a grin to Summer and Cam, seated in the back seat.

"Brace yourselves. Here comes the welcoming committee."

Cam frowned as his entire family began spilling out the front door like a swarm of locusts. "What're they all doing home?"

"I phoned ahead."

"Figures." With his arm and chest heavily bandaged, Cam stepped out of the car and caught Summer's hand.

"Cameron." Kate led the charge, stopping just short of hugging him to death. "Chris said you'd been shot."

"Just a flesh wound." Cam embraced her and awkwardly patted her back. "The doctor said I'll be fine in a couple of days."

Micah and Pru gathered around.

"Been a few years since you got down and dirty, bro." Micah clapped him on the back.

Cam grinned. "Yeah. Played hell on my custom-made suit."

Donovan had Taylor on his shoulders, his arm around Andi. She, in turn, had her arm around Cory, holding on tightly.

Donovan gave his brother a high five. "Fighting's like riding a bike. You never forget."

"So I've discovered." Imitating his older brothers, Cam put his good arm around Summer and drew her close. "You should've seen Goody Two-shoes here. She had her first lesson in street fighting."

Donovan glanced at Chris. "According to our brother-in-law, you're the real hero of the day, Summer."

Embarrassed, she shook her head. "You're wrong. Cam was the one who saved us all. You should have seen him. He was so cool and calm. If it hadn't been for him..." Her words trailed off as Kieran Lassiter headed toward them.

"So, boyo." Kieran caught his grandson in a fierce bear hug, which had Cam wincing. "You played it smart."

"Yeah. Just like you taught me, Pop."

The old man turned, still holding onto his grandson. "And the lass?"

"With a few lessons, I think she's got the makings of a good brawler."

"I'm proud of you, lass. Proud of both of you. Come on. Let's take this inside." He led them up the stairs just as Bren poked her head out the door.

"Hurry up. Cam, you've made the six o'clock news."

The family gathered around the television, watching as Alfonso's face appeared on the screen. The story unfolded, with the announcement that his wife had confessed her part in a scheme to make her innocent husband pay for the crime committed by her lover. A reporter was shown standing with a beaming Tio and his weeping grandmother as they spoke by phone with Alfonso in prison, where the warden had expressed his confidence that prisoner Alfonso Johnson would soon be a free man. Thanks, he added, to Cameron Lassiter, a brilliant young lawyer who was making a name for himself by working to free innocent prisoners.

The reporter went on to proclaim that the same lawyer, in the employ of Stern Hayes Wheatley, had just won the largest settlement in history for their client Lou Carlson in his suit against the McGonnagle Corporation. McGonnagle, fearing Cameron Lassiter's reputation, had relented and agreed to the settlement.

The great room exploded with cheers and shouting.

Minutes later the entire family retired to the kitchen. While Micah popped the cork on a bottle of champagne, and Bren passed around tulip glasses, they fell into the familiar routine of preparing an evening meal.

Summer stood to one side watching. Everyone, it seemed, knew, without being told, exactly what needed to be sliced, stirred, arranged.

Cam walked over to hand her a glass of champagne. Seeing the pensive look in her eyes, he tipped her chin. ''What's wrong?''

"Nothing." She shrugged. "Your family looks so...together."

"You think so?" He glanced around, then leaned close to whisper, "You wouldn't have thought that a few years ago. Micah and Pru would have been voted the couple least likely to get together. She's the daughter of one of the richest men in the country, and Micah's a working stiff. Then there's Donovan and Andi. He's a complete loner, and she and her kids were a package deal. Bren and Chris found themselves in a public debate on opposite sides of a police brutality issue." He took the glass from her hands, set it on the table and stared into her eyes. "Then there's you and me."

"What about us?"

"Yeah. That's what I'm wondering." Seeing that the others had grown unusually quiet, he caught her hand. "Come on."

As he started leading her across the room she pulled back. "Where are we going?"

"Away from big ears. My family has a history of eavesdropping." While the others continued with their chores, he opened the back door and led her toward the basketball hoop. He stopped and balanced the basketball in his good hand.

She eyed it, then him. "Is this some sort of a family ritual?"

He grinned. "Yeah. Pop taught us to bring our frustrations to the hoop."

"You're frustrated?"

"Yeah. I've got some…issues to deal with." Without looking at the hoop he tossed the ball one-handed behind him. It ringed the basket, then dropped through.

She blinked in surprise. "Lucky shot."

"Yeah. What are the odds I can do it again?" He caught the ball on the first bounce.

"Not very good, I'd say."

"Would you? Okay. Why don't I try again? But first, how about a little bet, to make it interesting."

She narrowed her eyes. "What's the bet?"

"If I make it, you'll agree to help me decorate my place."

"You already have a decorator."

"Had. I fired her and her firm."

"Why?"

"I realized what was wrong with my house. It was perfect. Painted perfect colors. Filled with perfect furniture. But it wasn't a home." He balanced the ball in his hand, while studying her eyes. "It needs you, Summer. And so do I. If I make the basket, will you marry me?"

She started to laugh, then realized he was serious. "And if you don't make it?"

He shrugged. "I'll leave that up to you."

She stared at him, then allowed a slow, easy smile to curve her lips. "You mean I can demand anything I want? Even if it's something really horrible?"

He nodded. "You could even insist that I propose to you in front of my entire family."

"That's pretty horrible, all right." She frowned. "Maybe I'm not interested in a proposal."

"You're a lousy liar. Besides, it doesn't matter. I am. Deal?"

She smiled, then nodded.

He continued looking at her as he tossed the ball behind him. Drawing her close, he brushed his mouth over hers.

"Wait." She pushed a little away. "I want to see who wins."

As the ball dropped cleanly through the hoop, her laughter was warm and musical on the evening air. She wrapped her arms around his neck and offered her mouth. "How did you know you'd win?"

"I couldn't lose. I've been practicing that shot since I was a kid. I always knew one day it would come in handy. Now you have to marry me."

"As you knew I would, since I always honor my debts."

He took the kiss deeper and murmured against her mouth, "I was counting on that."

"You're too smart for your own good."

"That's what Pop told me a long time ago." He felt the warmth of her kiss sliding lazily through his veins. "Let's get out of here and go back to my place."

"It's still a mess."

"All right then. Your place."

"Mmm." She held on, loving the way she felt in his arms. "I could be persuaded."

Just then they heard the sound of cheering and saw his entire family gathered in the big bay window, holding up their glasses of champagne in a toast. Minutes later they came streaming out the back door and down the steps to offer their congratulations to the happy couple.

As Cam and Summer were surrounded by laughing, cheering family, Kieran dropped an arm around his daughter-in-law's shoulders and drew her a little aside. "It looks like we did it, Katie girl. We're seeing the last of our chicks leave the nest."

Despite the lump in her throat, Kate Lassiter was smiling. "She's perfect for him, isn't she?"

"That she is." The old lion brushed a kiss over her cheek, tasting the salt of her tears. "Almost as perfect as you were for my Riordan."

She turned to him with shining eyes. "Maybe we'd better brace ourselves. Think you're ready for the next generation of Lassiters?"

"More than ready." He kissed the top of her head and studied the happy couple, surrounded by their laughing, chattering family. "You know something, Katie girl? Despite all the pain that brought us to this point in our lives, I wouldn't have missed a minute of it." His voice was a bit rough and scratchy, from the lump threatening to choke him. "Not a single minute of it."

* * * * *

In June 2002

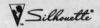

INTIMATE MOMENTS™

and
USA Today bestselling author

CANDACE CAMP

invite you to visit

A Little Town in TEXAS

with

SMOOTH-TALKING TEXAN (IM #1153)

Attorney Lisa Mendoza was fighting to save a young man's life.
Quinn Sutton was fighting for *her*.

Could a small-town sheriff have just what this big-city lawyer
was searching for?

Spend some time in A Little Town in Texas.
Where love runs deep in every heart.

And in case you missed
HARD-HEADED TEXAN (IM #1081)
you can order your own copy.